U0165852

口說日常生活英文片語會話

◎ 王仁癸 著 ◎

書泉出版社 印行

Preface 序言 PART

目前臺灣英文片語書的造句大多屬於學術性語言，對於口語生活造句極少，再加上國內各種大型考試都已加考口說測驗，口說的日常生活英文能力越顯重要。於是筆者以片語為主，展開場景式的對話，將一些相關的片語彙集在一起，讓讀者瞭解在哪種場景下會出現哪些片語，這樣就較能掌握住口說語言的核心關鍵概念。

本書為實用性的口說生活片語書，熟習本書的單字、例句與回答技巧，無形中可讓讀者能輕易地用片語來描述人、事、物，且書中的會話皆是標準美式口說表達，其單字與例句幾乎完全符合美國生活常用語言形式，這將有助於培養美語思維。

這本書的最大特點，除了實用性與場景性之外，就在其豐富內容所具有的創新性。首先，片語的選擇皆為口說生活常用片語，將有利於口說能力的培養；其次，編排以生活中的「食、衣、住、行、育、樂」六大單元來編排，每一單元內再分為不同的場景，有利於讀者根據自己的學習需求，優先選擇不同單元與場景來學習；第三，場景中的會話例句豐富，為原汁原味的道地美式口語。

在熟習本書後，將有助於各位口語溝通能力的增強，同時在一些國內考試聽力與口說考試中將會有明顯的進步。最後，非常感謝書泉圖書的鼎力相助，讓本書得以順利出版。

王仁癸

PART 目錄 Contents

Contents 目錄

PART

PART 1

第1單元

食生活片語

01 飲食評價場景

02 飲料場景

03 餐廳場景

04 付帳場景

05 減肥場景

06 飲食場景

07 家裡飲食場景

08 其他食場景

PART

01 飲食評價場景

be rich with 富含

A：You should eat more soybeans.

B：Yes, I should. They're rich with vitamins.

A：你應該多吃大豆。

B：沒錯，我應該多吃，它們富含維他命。

be rich with 和 be rich in 意思差不多，但 be rich in 強調「本身具有」，而 be rich with 只是強調「有」。

heavily seasoned 味道很重

指食物含有大量的調味料。

A：The meat tasted heavily seasoned.

B：Sure. The flavor was heavy.

A：這肉品嚐起來味道很重。

B：沒錯，味道很重。

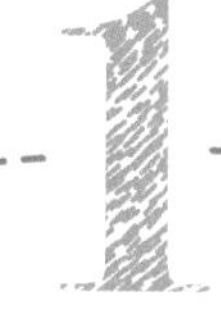

hit the spot 很好吃

指飲食口味恰到好處，表示好吃或好喝的意思。

A: Can you recommend what to have?

B: Well, you should try the apple pie. It really hits the spot.

A: 你能推薦一下吃什麼好呢？

B: 嗯，你應該嚐點蘋果派，它真的很好吃。

light meal 清淡的食物

指吃得少而清淡的一頓飯，有時候中文翻譯為「便餐」。

A: It's time for lunch. I want to have a light meal.

B: I know a good place where we can eat.

A: 吃午餐時間到了，我想吃點清淡的食物。

B: 我知道有一間好餐廳，我們可以去那裡吃。

lightly seasoned 味道很淡

A：I wonder what this soup tastes like.

B：I tried it. It is lightly seasoned.

A：我想知道湯的味道。

B：我喝過，它的味道很淡。

mouth-watering 很好吃

直譯爲「流口水」，只有食物好吃，才會有此現象。

A：The chocolate looks mouth-watering.

B：It really does.

A：巧克力看起來很好吃。

B：沒有錯。

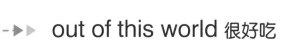

out of this world 很好吃

指食物只有天上才有，表示好吃。

A: I'm starving. Where are we going to eat?

B: I know one restaurant where the food is out of this world.

A: 我很餓，我們到哪裡吃飯呢？

B: 我知道有家餐廳，那裡的食物非常好吃。

square meal 豐盛飲食

指食物必須豐盛與營養。

A: My doctor says I eat too much junk food.

B: What you need is a good square meal, that's much more wholesome.

A: 我的醫生說我吃太多垃圾食物了。

B: 你需要的是吃更有益健康的豐盛飲食。

PART

to sb.'s liking 好吃

指合某人口味，強調食物好吃。

A: Have you tried the steak? It's to my liking.

B: It looks tasty, but I'm a vegetarian.

A: 你吃過這牛排嗎？它很好吃。

B: 它看起來很好吃，但是我吃素。

to sb.'s taste 合某人口味

A: Would you like some stinky tofu?

B: No, thanks. It's not really to my taste.

A: 你要吃點臭豆腐嗎？

B: 不，謝謝，它不合我的口味。

well-cooked 煮熟

A：The lamb looks well-cooked.

B：Wow, it must be very delicious.

A：羊肉看起來煮熟了。

B：哇，一定非常好吃。

whet sb.'s appetite 引起某人的食欲

A：I am making apple pies for our lunch.

B：It sort of whets my appetite. I can't wait for lunch.

A：我正在做蘋果派當做我們的中餐。

B：它有點引起我的食欲，我等不及要吃中餐了。

補充

whet sb.'s appetite 有「吸引某人的興趣」的意思，如 The book whets my appetite to explore the culture of the west. 這本書引起我探討西方文化的興趣。

PART

02 飲料場景

a cup of Joe 一杯咖啡

Joe 或 Java 在英文飲料場景中，是指咖啡。

A：Do you want a cup of tea or Joe?

B：A cup of Joe, please.

A：你想要喝一杯茶或咖啡？

B：請給我一杯咖啡。

a cup of Joe = a cup of Java = a cup of coffee

a tall milk shake 一杯大奶昔

tall 通常指較高的意思，飲料因爲高才會大杯。

A：What would you like to order?

B：I want a tall milk shake and a large fries.

A：你想要點什麼？
B：我想要一杯大奶昔和一份大薯條。

be addicted to 喜歡

指喜歡上某物，而且又上癮。

A：I'm addicted to coffee. I hardly wake up all day without coffee.

B：I guess you like to drink a cup of black coffee.

A：我喜歡喝咖啡，沒有喝咖啡，我整天幾乎都不清醒。
B：我想你較喜歡喝黑咖啡。

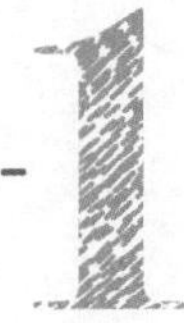

PART

be off caffeine 不能沾咖啡因

此片語中的 off 是指斷絕或不再喜歡的意思。

A：Would you like a cup of coffee?

B：I'm off caffeine, so no coffee for me.

A：你想要喝一杯咖啡嗎？

B：我不能碰咖啡因，所以我不喝咖啡。

Bottoms up 乾杯

A：Today is my birthday. Everyone, a toast.

B：Bottoms up.

A：今天是我生日，敬大家一杯酒。

B：乾杯。

care for 喜歡

A：Would you like cakes?

B：I don't care much for them.

A：你想吃蛋糕嗎？

B：我不太喜歡吃蛋糕。

caffeine free 不含咖啡因

解說

此片語中的 free，是強調「沒有」的意思。

A：I can't drink too much coffee, or I can't fall asleep.

B：You can drink the flower tea. It is caffeine free.

A：我不能喝太多咖啡，否則我無法入睡。

B：你可以喝花茶，它不含咖啡因。

1 PART

discuss sth. over coffee 邊喝咖啡邊討論某事

A: This article is worth discussing.

B: Sure. Maybe we can discuss it over coffee.

A: 這篇文章很值得討論。

B: 沒錯，或許我們可以一邊喝咖啡一邊討論。

free refill 免費續杯

A: Are there free refills on the coke?

B: Yes, there are.

A: 可樂有免費續杯嗎？

B: 有。

get a refill 續杯

A: Can I get a refill of coffee?

B：This coffee is bottomless.

A：咖啡可以續杯嗎？
B：這咖啡是可以續杯的。

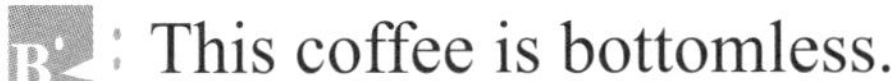

go overboard 過量

解說
原本是過分愛好的意思，用在飲料場景中，指過量的意思。

A：Drinking coffee always relaxes me.

B：Sure. Just don't go overboard.

A：喝咖啡總是讓我放輕鬆。
B：沒錯，只是不要喝過量。

pick-me-up 提神飲料

解說
指含有令人興奮作用的飲料。

A: I drink a cup of coffee at breakfast every day.

B: Coffee is your pick-me-up, I know.

A: 我每天早餐都喝一杯咖啡。

B: 我知道，咖啡是你的提神飲料。

grind coffee 現磨咖啡，blend coffee 混合咖啡，instant coffee 即溶咖啡。

▶▶ wake up 醒來

指覺醒、喚醒或活躍起來。

A: I can't seem to wake up in the morning without coffee at breakfast.

B: Well, you shouldn't drink too much or it will stain your teeth.

A: 我早上沒喝咖啡就似乎無法醒來。

B: 嗯，你不該喝太多，否則會弄黑你的牙齒。

be in charge of 負責

A: I'm so dissatisfied with the service here that I have a complaint to make.

B: I'm in charge of the restaurant when the manager is not available.

A: 我很不滿意這裡的服務，因此我要投訴。

B: 當經理不在時，由我負責這間餐廳。

be particular about 對…挑剔

A: Are you particular about food?

B: Look at the empty plates on the table. Does that answer your question?

A: 你對食物很挑剔嗎？

B: 看看桌上的空盤子，它有回答你的問題嗎？

be particular about = be picky about

be picky about 對…挑剔

A: The buffet was my favorite place during the trip.

B: But I know you are picky about food.

A: 在旅行時，自助餐廳是我最喜歡去的地方。
B: 但是我知道你對食物很挑剔。

book a table 訂位

A: I'd like to book a table for four at six tonight.

B: I'm sorry. We are fully booked.

A: 我想要預訂今晚六點4個人的座位。
B: 抱歉，座位都訂滿了。

come with 附贈

A: What comes with my meal?

B: A coke and a large fries.

A：我的餐點會附贈什麼呢？
B：一杯可樂與一份大薯條。

come with 有「伴隨…發生」的意思，如 It's a trend that the cell phone comes with no contract to attract consumers because of dog eat dog. 因為競爭非常激烈，以不簽約手機來吸引消費者是一個趨勢。

cup of tea 喜愛的人或事物

A：Would you prefer crab or lobster?

B：Lobster is my cup of tea.

A：你較喜歡吃螃蟹或是龍蝦呢？
B：龍蝦是我的最愛。

doggy bag 打包

doggy bag 是食物袋，引申為「打包」的意思。

A: May I have a doggy bag?

B: Of course. Let me help you to pack the left-overs in the doggy bag.

A: 我可以打包嗎？
B: 當然可以，我幫你把剩菜打包起來。

dine out 外出吃飯

dine 吃飯。

A: I would like to dine out tonight.

B: Do you have any particular restaurant in mind?

A: 今晚我想要外出吃飯。
B: 你有沒有特別想到怎樣的餐廳呢？

dine out = eat out

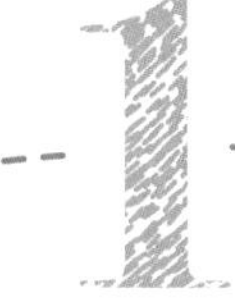

drive-in restaurant 得來速餐廳

就是免下車的餐廳，指消費者購買食物後，在車上享用，類似麥當勞得來速；而此片語中的drive-in爲「免下車」的意思。

A: Could you tell me where the nearest drive-in restaurant is?

B: I think it's about two kilometers down there.

A: 你可以告訴我最近的得來速餐廳在哪裡嗎？

B: 我想那裡大約是南下兩公里。

fancy restaurant 豪華餐廳

A: What are you up to tonight?

B: We're off to a fancy restaurant for dining.

A: 你們今晚要做什麼呢？

B: 我們要前往一家豪華餐廳用餐。

fancy restaurant = elegant restaurant

PART

go with 附贈

A：Does the meal come with a soda?

B：No, it doesn't go with a soda.

A：這餐點有附贈汽水嗎？
B：不，沒有附贈汽水。

go with = come with

fill up 客滿

A：Let's go to that new restaurant.

B：I heard that restaurant fills up quickly lately.

A：我們去那家新開的餐廳。
B：我聽說最近那家餐廳很快就會客滿。

for a change 改變一下

解說

此片語必須放在句尾。

A: Every year we celebrate Thanksgiving at home.

B: Why don't you go somewhere else for a change?

A: 每年我們都在家裡慶祝感恩節。

B: 你們為什麼不改變一下去別的地方呢？

greasy spoon 廉價餐館

解說

指供應廉價食物，但是衛生環境有點髒的餐館。

A: Let's go to a greasy spoon to eat something.

B: I won't argue with that idea.

A: 我們去廉價餐館吃些東西吧。

B: 我同意。

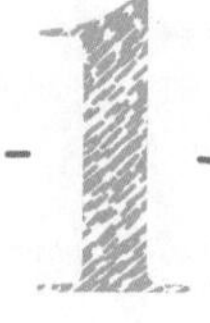

PART

have a problem with 對…不滿

指對什麼有問題、麻煩或不滿。

A: I have a big problem with that waiter.

B: What's the beef?

A: 我對那位服務生很不滿。
B: 你在不滿什麼呢？

house specialty 招牌菜

A: What is the house specialty?

B: It's our homemade baked apple pie.

A: 這裡的招牌菜是什麼？
B: 我們自家烤的蘋果派。

instead of 是…而不是

A：Waiter, I ordered spaghetti instead of pizza.

B：Sorry. I'll see to it straight away.

A：服務生，我點的是義大利麵而不是比薩。

B：對不起，我馬上處理。

invite to 邀請

A：I invited Tom to dinner tonight.

B：Ok, but the restaurant said we need to make reservation one week in advance.

A：我邀請湯姆今晚來吃晚餐。

B：很好啊，但是這家餐廳說，我們需要在一週前預約。

junk food 速食食物

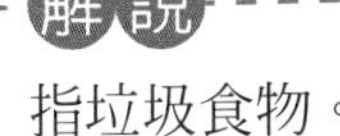

解說

指垃圾食物。

A : As a rule, I choose to eat junk food.

B : I wish I had a healthier lifestyle.

A : 通常我選擇去吃速食食物。

B : 我要是有一個更健康的生活方式就好了。

as a rule = usually；junk food = unhealthy food

keep an eye out for sb. 等待某人的來臨

keep an eye out for sb. 爲關注某人的出現，這裡引申爲等待某人的來臨。

A : I will have to meet you at the restaurant tonight.

B : Ok, I'll keep an eye out for you.

A : 我今晚一定會在餐廳跟你見面。

B : 好的，我會等待你的來臨。

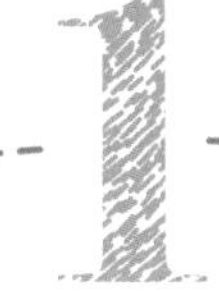

main course 主菜

A：What would you like for your main course, sir?

B：I think I'll have the steak.

A：先生，主菜你想要吃什麼？
B：我想我要吃牛排。

main course = main dish = entree

make a reservation 預訂

A：We can't get in without reservation.

B：Next time we had better make a reservation in advance.

A：沒有預訂，我們進不去。
B：下次，我們最好提前預訂。

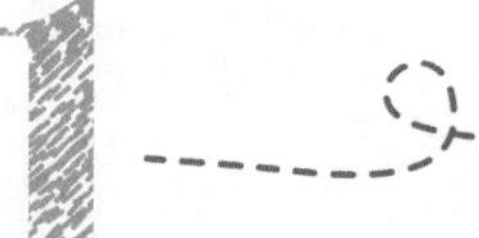

next to 在…旁邊

A：May I sit next to you at dinner?

B：No, my boyfriend will be sitting next to me.

A：吃晚飯時，我可以坐在你旁邊嗎？
B：不行，我男朋友會坐在我旁邊。

on the house 免費

指主人招待。

A：Tonight, drinks are on the house.

B：What's the special occasion?

A：今晚，飲料免費。
B：是什麼特別的日子呢？

on the side 另外

A：What would you like to order for dinner?

B：I'll have a steak and a salad on the side, please.

A：你晚餐想要點什麼？
B：我要一份牛排，另外加一份沙拉。

put up 張貼

指公布消息來吸引別人注意。

A：Had you seen the poster they just put up in the cafeteria?

B：Yes, I had. It just didn't go with the colors in the cafeteria.

A：你有看到自助餐廳裡才張貼沒多久的海報嗎？
B：有啊，我有看到，只是它跟自助餐裡面的顏色不搭配。

PART

ready to order 準備點菜

A: Are you ready to order?

B: Not yet, sorry. Could you give us five minutes, please?

A: 你準備點菜了嗎？

B: 抱歉，還沒有，請你給我們5分鐘，好嗎？

snack bar 小吃店

A: I'm going to the snack bar to eat tasty food and drink a cup of coffee. Would you like to come along?

B: I can't think of anything I'd rather do right now.

A: 我正要去小吃店吃美味食物和喝一杯咖啡，你想不想一起去呢？

B: 我從現在就不想做別的事情了。（暗示：要去小吃店）

see to 處理

解說

此片語是強調負責任與處理事情的意思。

A: You seem to have served me the wrong dish.

B: Sorry, I'll see to it right now.

A: 你似乎上錯菜了。

B: 抱歉，我會馬上處理此事。

補充

see to = take care of

start off 開始

A: Are you ready to order your meals?

B: Let's start off with some drinks first.

A: 你準備好點餐了嗎？

B: 我們先從點些飲料開始吧。

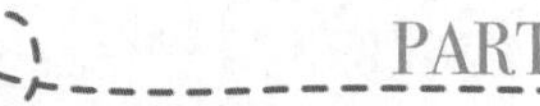

take care of 處理

A: The platter is broken.

B: Don’t worry. I’ll take care of it straight away.

A: 大淺盤破了。

B: 不要擔心，我會立即處理。

take out 外帶

A: Is that to eat in or to take out?

B: Take out, please.

A: 你是內用還是外帶呢？

B: 外帶。

think much of 高度評價

A: Why don’t we eat at this restaurant?

B: To tell you the truth, I don’t think much of the food in this restaurant.

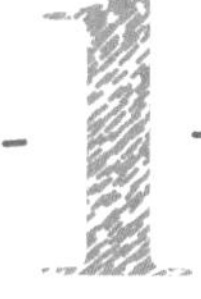

A：我們為什麼不在這家餐廳吃飯呢？

B：老實跟你說，我對這家餐廳的食物沒有好的評價。

unhealthy food 垃圾食物

A：How do you keep healthy?

B：Cutting unhealthy food out of my diet is a must.

A：你是如何保持身體健康呢？

B：飲食中減少垃圾食物是必須的條件。

be a must 必須的條件。

wait on 招待

A：Is there anyone here to serve us?

B：This waitress will wait on you.

A：這兒有人招待我們嗎？
B：這位女服務生會招待你們。

serve = attend on = wait on

well done 全熟

A：How would you like your steak?

B：Well done, please.

A：你的牛排要幾分熟？
B：全熟。

medium 五分熟，rare 全生。

04 付帳場景

come to 總共

A：Check, please?

B：That comes to 100 dollars.

A：請結帳。

B：總共100美元。

補充

口語中 May I have the check, please? 會經常省略 May I have the，直接以 check, please 來表示請結帳。

credit card 信用卡

A：How would you like to pay?

B：May I use my credit card?

A：你想怎樣付帳呢？

B：我能用信用卡結帳嗎？

1 PART

go Dutch 各付各的

A：I'll buy you dinner.

B：Don't be silly. Let's go Dutch.

A：我請你吃晚餐。

B：別傻了，讓我們各付各的吧。

補充

go Dutch = Dutch treat

it's on sb. 由某人請客

A：Why don't we go Dutch?

B：That's ok. It's on me.

A：我們為什麼不各付各的？

B：不用，我請客。

補充

這裡的 That's ok 有拒絕的意思，表示不要各付各的；若回答是 ok 時，那就表示各付各的。

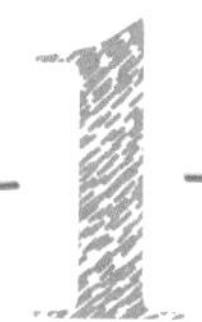

keep the change 零錢不用找

把零錢留著，就是說不用找的意思。

A: The total is 97 dollars, please.

B: Here's 100 dollars. Keep the change.

A: 全部97美元。

B: 這裡是100美元，零錢不用找。

on credit 賒帳

A: Can I buy the furniture on credit?

B: Yes, you can.

A: 我可以賒帳買這套家具嗎？

B: 可以。

by check 用支票；in cash 用現金。

PART

pick up the tab 付帳

A: You don't have to pay the bill today. I'll pick up the tab.

B: Thanks, I'll get in next time.

A: 今天你不用付這帳單，我來付帳。

B: 謝謝，下次我請客。

補充

pick up the tab = pick up the bill

separate checks 分開付帳

A: Do you want to pay with separate checks?

B: Together, please.

A: 你想要分開付帳嗎？

B: 一起付，謝謝。

補充

separate checks = separate bills

share the expense 各自付帳

A : Shall we share the expense this time?

B : Oh, no. It's on me.

A：這次我們各自付帳嗎？

B：不，我請客。

split the check 各付各的

A : Let me buy you a drink.

B : No, let's split the check.

A：我請你喝一杯飲料吧。

B：不，我們各付各的吧。

stand treat 請客

A : Who is going to stand treat?

B : I stand treat today.

A：誰請客？
B：今天我請客。

take care of 付帳

take care of 後面接 bill 或 check，在英文口語的解釋，是「付帳」的意思。

A：I will take care of the bill.

B：Thank you.

A：我來付帳。
B：謝謝你。

05 減肥場景

burn off 燃燒

解說

burn off 不僅有「燒掉」的意思，也有「消耗」的意思，如 burn off energy 消耗能源、burn off calories 消耗卡路里。

A: Why is your belly fat gone?

B: I have been exercising lately to burn off my excess fat.

A: 你的腹部贅肉為什麼消失了呢？

B: 我最近一直在鍛鍊身體，來燃燒我過多的脂肪。

cut back on 減少

A: I'm having trouble fitting into my jeans.

B: I think you should cut back on the fatty foods.

A: 我的牛仔褲穿不下去了。

B: 我認為你應該減少吃高脂食物。

PART

cut out 停止

A: Cutting out fattening food is important to keep fit.

B: I'm no fool. I have already knew that.

A: 停止吃油膩食物對保持健康是重要的。

B: 我不是傻子，我早就知道了。

fitness center 健身中心

A: How do you keep in such good shape?

B: I go to the fitness center 5 days a week.

A: 你是如何保持這麼好的身材呢？

B: 我一週有五天去健身中心。

fitness center = gym；keep in good shape = stay in good shape，且 shape 前面不可有 the 與 a。

gain some pounds 長胖

指增加一些體重。

A：You look like you've been gaining some pounds.

B：I know. I need to stop eating junk foods.

A：你看起來好像長胖了。

B：我知道，我得停止吃垃圾食物。

gain some pounds = gain some weight = put on some weight

keep in shape 保持身材

A：The roast turkey looks like yummy. Are you going to have some with us?

B：Well, I want to keep in shape, but Thanksgiving Day only comes once a year.

A：這烤火雞看起來很美味，你要跟我們一起吃嗎？

B：嗯，我想要保持身材，但是感恩節一年只有一次。

lose weight 減肥

A：I think avoiding high-calorie foods is the best way to lose some weight.

B：Yeah. It works and can keep you away from the doctor.

A：我認為避免吃高卡路里食品是最好的減肥方法。

B：沒錯，該方法有效，能讓你遠離疾病。

on a diet 節食

指控制飲食來減肥塑身。

A：You should eat more meat.

B：Thanks. But I'm on a diet.

A：你應該多吃一些肉。
B：謝謝，但是我正在節食。

put on weight 體重增加

A：I've put on some weight lately. I think I need to go on a diet.

B：That's a good idea. You have to try to limit your meat intake.

A：最近我體重增加一些，我想我需要節食。
B：那是個好主意，你必須設法限制肉的攝取。

slim down 減肥

解說

slim 使…體重減輕。

A: Summer is approaching and I want to slim down a bit, so I can fit into my swimsuit.

B: You'd better get started on a diet then.

A: 夏天來臨了，我要稍微減肥，這樣我就能穿上我的泳裝。

B: 那麼你最好要開始節食。

▶▶ watch sb.'s diet 減肥

注意某人飲食，意指要減肥。

A: I cannot fit into my pants anymore.

B: I guess you should start watching your diet.

A: 我再也穿不下我的褲子。

B: 我想你應該開始減肥。

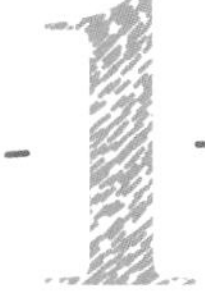

watch sb.'s figure 減肥

控制某人身材，意指要減肥。

A: Would you like to go with us for a snack a little later?

B: No snack for me, thanks. I'm watching my figure.

A: 待會兒你願意跟我們去吃點心嗎？

B: 我不吃點心，謝謝，我正在減肥。

06 飲食場景

▶▶ dig in 開始大吃

A: Wow, strawberry-flavored ice cream. It looks yummy.

B: Let's dig in.

A: 哇，草莓口味的冰淇淋，它看起來很好吃。

B: 讓我們開始大吃吧。

▶▶ eat like a horse 食量很大

A: How is your appetite today?

B: I could eat like a horse.

A: 今天你胃口如何？

B: 我食量很大。

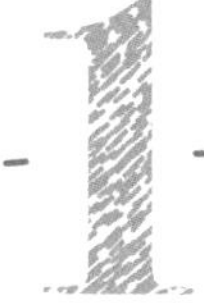

eat like a sparrow 食量很小

A：You eat like a sparrow and should eat more for health.

B：Yes, I know, but I'm watching my figure.

A：你食量很小，為了健康要多吃一點。

B：是的，我知道，但是我正在減肥。

Don't mind if I do. 我就不客氣了

其中文意思爲「如果我這樣做的話，請不要介意」，其語意爲表示非常有禮貌地接受別人提供的邀請、恩惠或幫助等等。

A：Would you like some dessert?

B：Thank you. Don't mind if I do.

A：你想吃點甜點嗎？

B：謝謝，那我就不客氣了。

PART

fix a snack 吃點東西

指隨便吃點零食。

A: I'm really hungry after my long work out.

B: You can fix a snack in the kitchen.

A: 長時間的運動後，我很餓。

B: 你可以在廚房裡吃點東西。

grab a bite to eat 吃點東西

A: Let's grab a bite to eat after the concert.

B: That sounds like a good idea. I'm starving now.

A: 在音樂會後，我們去吃點東西吧。

B: 這主意聽起來不錯，現在我快餓死了。

grab a bite to eat = get a bite to eat = have a bite to eat

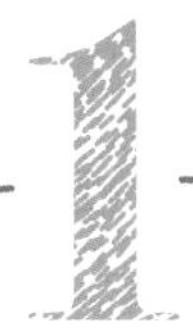

▶▶ grab a snack 隨便吃一吃

指隨便吃點東西。

A：Let's grab a snack at the café.

B：Yeah, it sounds like a good idea to me.

A：我們在簡餐店隨便吃一吃吧。

B：好啊，這個主意聽起來不錯。

▶▶ have a sweet tooth 喜歡吃甜食

sweet tooth 是喜歡吃甜的，而類似的片語 meat tooth 是喜歡吃肉。

A：Do you have a sweet tooth?

B：Yes, the vanilla ice cream is my favorite flavor, but I would never substitute sweets for a real meal.

PART

A：你喜歡吃甜食嗎？

B：對，香草冰淇淋是我最喜歡的口味，但是我從不吃甜食來替代正餐。

▶▶ have the stomach for 喜歡

對什麼食物都有胃口，表示喜歡的意思。

A：Do you enjoy fish and chips?

B：I don't really have the stomach for it.

A：你喜歡吃炸魚和薯條嗎？

B：我並不喜歡吃。

補充

have no stomach for 不喜歡。

in line 排隊

A: I saw you standing in line for snacks.

B: Yes, it took forever to get through it.

A: 我看見你在排隊買小吃。
B: 沒錯，花了很多時間才買到。

run down to 去

指去某地方一趟，或去做某事情，強調人或物之間的延伸性。

A: I have to run down to the store and buy something for dinner.

B: Don't forget to buy some milk.

A: 我必須去商店買東西做晚餐。
B: 不要忘記買些牛奶。

run down to = go down to

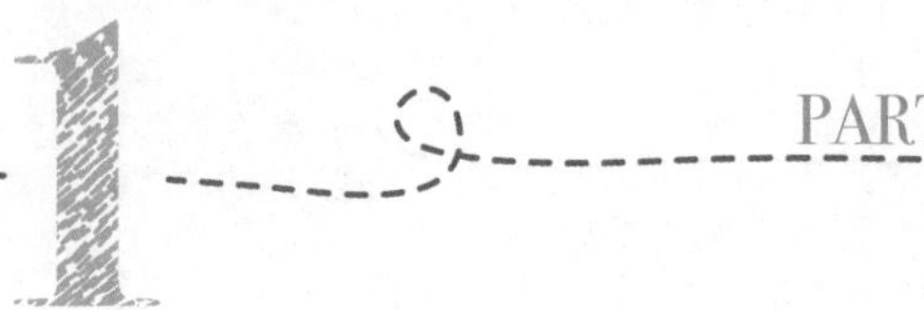

The more, the merrier. 人越多，越熱鬧

A: May I bring my parents to your picnic?

B: Yes. The more, the merrier.

A: 我可以帶我的雙親參加你的野餐嗎？

B: 可以，人越多，越熱鬧。

be low on 缺乏

A：I'm going to the grocery store. Need anything?

B：Well, I'm low on sugar.

A：我要去雜貨店，你有需要任何東西嗎？
B：嗯，我缺乏糖。

be stuffed 吃飽

A：You may go ahead and serve desserts.

B：Let's wait a while. I am stuffed now.

A：你可以先上甜點。
B：等一會兒吧，我現在吃很飽。

do the cooking 做飯

A：It's your turn to do the cooking tonight.

B：Ok, I'll cook you my specialty, beans on toast.

A：今晚輪到你做飯。

B：沒錯，我會煮我的「烤土司豆子」招牌菜給你吃。

cooking 烹飪，cooker 廚具，cook 廚師。

▸▸ empty handed 空手的

A：I don't think I should go to his home for dinner empty handed.

B：You could pick up some ice cream for him. Vanilla is his favorite ice cream flavor.

A：我想我不應該空手去他家吃晚餐。

B：你可以帶些冰淇淋給他，香草是他最喜歡的冰淇淋口味。

drink up 喝完

A：Drink up your milk. It's time for you to go to bed.

B：I know. But my assignment isn't finished.

A：把你的牛奶喝完，你該去睡覺的時間到了。

B：我知道，但我的作業還沒寫完。

eat up 是吃光。

family reunion dinner 團圓飯

A：Chinese New Year's Eve is a time for a family reunion dinner.

B：I know. That's my favorite festival and I can enjoy a delicious dinner.

A：農曆年除夕夜是團圓飯的時刻。

B：我知道，那是我喜愛的節日，我能享受一頓美味的晚餐。

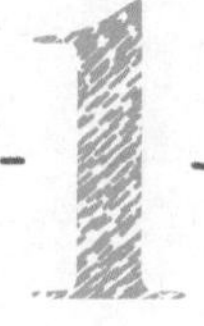

PART

go bad 變質

指食物變質或變壞。

A：The milk smells like it has gone bad.

B：I think you have kept it too long and it cannot be drunk.

A：這牛奶聞起來像是變質了。

B：我想你放的時間太長了，不能再喝了。

go bad = go off

have another commitment 有約

A：Would you like to come over for dinner tonight?

B：Unfortunately, I have another commitment.

A：你今晚能過來吃晚餐嗎？

B：不幸的是，我另外有約。

home grown 自家種植的

自產的，常指水果，蔬菜等。

A：The vegetables are delicious.

B：Thank you. They're home grown.

A：這些蔬菜味道好極了。

B：謝謝，它們是自家種植的。

make it from scratch 自己做的

make it 是「做到」、「完成」的意思，from scratch 是「從無到有」的意思，而 make it from scratch 的意思就是從基本材料做起，一點點地將東西做成。

A：The pasta is delicious.

B：Thanks. My mom made it from scratch.

A：義大利麵很好吃。

B：謝謝，我媽媽自己做的。

PART

▸▸ make tea 泡茶

泡茶或泡咖啡的動詞都用 make。

A: Can you make tea, Mary?

B: Sure.

A: 瑪麗，你會泡茶嗎？

B: 當然會。

▸▸ set the table 擺設餐具

A: How many guests will be at the dinner?

B: Two guests. So you have to set the table for six.

A: 會有多少客人來吃晚餐呢？

B: 2位客人，所以你必須擺設6人份的餐具。

set the table = lay the table

talk with sb.'s mouth full

說話時滿嘴食物

A: We don't talk during the meal.

B: It is rude to talk with your mouth full.

A: 吃飯時，我們不說話。

B: 說話時滿嘴食物很不禮貌。

補充

talk with sb.'s mouth full = speak with sb.'s mouth full

08 其他食場景

be tired of 厭倦

A: I am really tired of the same old food every day.

B: I agree. The school should offer more variety.

A: 我很厭倦每天吃相同的食物。
B: 我同意，學校應該提供更多樣的食物。

be good for sb. 對某人有益

A: Eat up your greens. It is really good for you.

B: I know.

A: 把青菜吃完，它真的對你有益。
B: 我知道。

補充

be good for 有「能保持…有效」的意思，如 The gift certificate is good for 30 days from the issuing date. 禮券自發行日開始，有效使用30天。

have indigestion 消化不良

A: It's no wonder why you have indigestion, because you eat so fast.

B: Actually, I don't think it happens to me. I've got a healthy strong stomach, the doctor said.

A：難怪為什麼你會消化不良，因為你吃太快。

B：事實上，我不認為它會發生在我身上。醫生說，我有一個健康強壯的胃。

in season 盛產時期

A: The oranges look juicy. Let's buy them.

B: They are in season now, so the price is cheap.

A：橘子看起來汁很多，我們買橘子吧。

B：橘子現在是盛產時期，所以價錢便宜。

on special 特價優惠

就是以特價出售。

A: I heard the grapes are on special today only.

B: Let's go and buy some as early as possible.

A: 我聽說葡萄在特價優惠中，只限今天。

B: 我們趁早去買一些葡萄吧。

on top of sth. 除…外

A: I ate a burger and some French fries for dinner. On top of that, I had ice cream for dessert.

B: Oh, my goodness. You ate too much junk food.

A: 我晚餐吃一個漢堡和一些薯條，除此之外，我的甜點吃冰淇淋。

B: 哦，天啊，你吃太多垃圾食物了。

pick up 買

A: I need to get something from the store. I'll be right back.

B: Can you pick me up a Pepsi, while you're there?

A: 我需要去商店買些東西，馬上就回來。

B: 你到那以後，能幫我買一瓶百事可樂嗎？

be back 回來。

next to 除了

用在有程度上的順序。

A: Next to chocolate cake, apple pie is my favorite dessert.

B: My favorite is ice cream.

PART

A：除了巧克力蛋糕，蘋果派是我最喜歡的點心。

B：我最喜歡的點心是冰淇淋。

out of season 淡季

指海鮮蔬果不合季節，引申爲淡季。

A: Does your store sell strawberries?

B: Usually, yes. But they are currently out of season.

A：你們店裡有賣草莓嗎？

B：正常情況下，是有賣，但是現在是草莓的淡季。

補充

in season 正當盛產季節／應時的。

stock up 囤積

A：The supermarket is bankrupt. Now everything is fifty percent off.

B：In this case, we should stock up on groceries.

A：這家超市破產了，現在每樣東西都打五折。
B：在這種情況下，我們應該囤積食物。

there's nothing worse than 沒有比什麼還糟糕的事

A：Hey, Helen. Please try not to overcook my steak.

B：Sure, there's nothing worse than eating overcooked food.

A：嗨，海倫，請不要把我的牛排煮太熟。
B：好的，沒有事情比吃煮爛的食物還糟糕的事。

PART 

第
2
單元

衣生活片語

01 買衣服場景

02 穿衣服場景

03 衣服評價場景

PART

01 買衣服場景

▶▶ a good buy 便宜貨

通常指物美價廉。

A：I heard you bought that dress for only $50.00.

B：Yes, it was really a good buy.

A：我聽說你只花50元就買到那件衣服。
B：沒錯，那件衣服很便宜。

a good buy = a steal

▶▶ a good bargain 便宜貨

A：The shirt costs me only 5 bucks.

B：That's a good bargain.

A：這件襯衫只花了我5美元。
B：那很便宜。

be made of 由…製成

A：What is this shirt made of ?

B：It is made of cotton.

A：這件襯衫是由什麼製成的？

B：它是由棉布製成的。

be perfect with 搭配

指很適合。

A：The pink blouse is perfect with her skirt.

B：Yes, you're right about that.

A：這件粉紅色上衣和她的裙子很搭配。

B：沒錯，你說得對。

▶▶ become on 適合

指某物適合某人，可使某人更具有吸引力。

A: May I try on the clothes?

B: Sure. I think it's very becoming on you.

A: 我可以試穿這件衣服嗎？

B: 當然可以，我認為這件衣服非常適合你。

▶▶ bring back 帶回來

A: What a beautiful hat. It must be from New York.

B: No. My parents bring it back from San Francisco for me as my birthday present.

A: 多漂亮的帽子，一定來自紐約。

B: 不是，我的雙親把它從舊金山帶回來，當作我的生日禮物。

browse around 逛逛

指四處瀏覽看看。

A: All girls' clothes are half price at the department store now.

B: I don't have enough money to buy clothes. I just want to browse around.

A: 現在這家百貨公司所有女孩的衣服都是半價。

B: 我沒有足夠的錢買衣服，我只想去逛逛。

browse around = look around

cast on 披上

A: Your overcoat cast on you is really nice.

B: That is taken for granted.

A: 披在你身上的大衣很漂亮。

B: 那是當然的。

PART

▶▶ catch sb.'s eye 吸引某人的注意

指吸引某人注意，有喜歡的意思。

A：Look at the pink dress in the store window. It really catches my eye.

B：Well, if you like it that much, why don't you buy it?

A：看看商店櫥窗裡的粉紅色套裝，它很吸引我的注意。

B：嗯，如果你那麼喜歡，你為什麼不買呢？

▶▶ change for a larger size 換大一號的

A：I think the size is too small. Could I change it for a larger size?

B：Of course.

A：我想這尺寸太小了，我可以換大一號的嗎？

B：沒問題。

change for a smaller size 換小一號的

A: I don't think this dressy dress will fit me.

B: Well. If it is not your size, you can change it for a smaller size.

A: 我不認為這件漂亮衣服我穿得下。

B: 喔，如果不是你的尺寸，你可以換小一號的。

clearance sale 清倉大拍賣

A: I heard William's Sweater Shop is having a clearance sale tomorrow.

B: Great. That's just what I've been waiting for.

A: 我聽說明天威廉毛衣店會舉行清倉大拍賣。

B: 太好了，那正是我在等待的。

PART

▶▶ clothes don't match 衣服不搭配

A: Your clothes don't match.

B: I agree. I felt that the scarf doesn't match with my dress.

A: 你的衣服看起來不搭配。

B: 我同意。我覺得圍巾和我的套裝不搭配。

▶▶ give sb. a discount 給某人打折

A: Could you give me a discount from the clothes?

B: I would give you 10% discount for cash.

A: 你能在這件衣服上給我一個折扣嗎？

B: 現金付款，我給你九折優待。

▶▶ go with 搭配

A: Why are you returning the jacket?

B: I bought it to go with my grey trousers, but they don't really match.

A: 你為什麼要退掉這件夾克呢？

B: 我本來是買這件夾克來搭配我的灰色褲子，但是它們很不搭配。

have a sale 大拍賣

主詞必須爲店家，指店家進行銷售活動。

A: Have you heard about Hang Ten's store?

B: Yes. They are having a sale at the moment to reduce stock.

A: 你聽說過Hang Ten商店嗎？

B: 有，他們目前在舉辦大拍賣來減少存貨。

PART

▸▸ look around 逛逛

強調四處看看。

A：Welcome, sir. Is there anything you want to buy here?

B：I want to look around more first.

A：歡迎您，先生，您想要買點什麼東西嗎？

B：我想先逛逛再說。

▸▸ match with 與…搭配

A：That navy blue jacket matches well with your scarf.

B：Yes, that's why I bought it.

A：那件海軍藍夾克與你的圍巾很搭配。

B：沒錯，那就是我買它的原因。

next size down 小一號

A：The size 11 feels a little too loose. Do you have this in the next size down?

B：Yes, I'll bring you some smaller ones.

A：尺寸11號有點鬆，你有這種款式尺寸小一號的嗎？

B：有，我再拿小一碼的尺寸給你。

補充

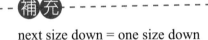

next size down = one size down

next size up 大一號

A：The jacket doesn't fit me.

B：You'd better get the next size up for it to feel comfortable.

A：這件夾克我穿不合身。

B：要想感到舒服，你最好買大一號的夾克。

next size up = one size up

off the rack 現成的

A: I want to get a custom-made suit to wear.

B: I usually buy my suits off the rack because it's cheaper.

A: 我想要買一套訂做的西服來穿。

B: 我通常買現成的西服，因為這樣比較便宜。

custom-made 訂製的。

on sale 拍賣

on sale 必須要以商品爲主詞。

A: Lots of things in the clothing department store down the street are on sale.

B：Sounds like an ideal time to buy a down jacket.

A：沿著這條街的服飾百貨公司，許多東西都正在拍賣。

B：聽起來好像正是買羽絨衣的好時機。

get money back 退錢

強調有購買行爲的償還。

A：The blouse faded the first time I washed it. I'd like you to get my money back.

B：Bring your receipt to customer service and they will refund your money.

A：這件襯衫我第一次洗就褪色了，我希望你退錢給我。

B：帶著你的收據去服務臺，他們會退錢給你。

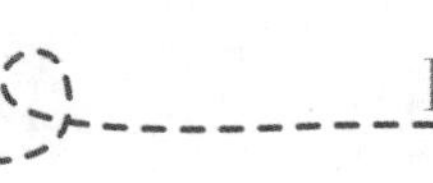

plan on 打算

A: What are you planning on buying at the new department store?

B: I will buy some shoes and some new trousers.

A: 你打算在這新開幕的百貨公司買什麼呢？

B: 我會買鞋子和新褲子。

pick out 挑選

A: Could you help me pick out an evening gown, please?

B: Certainly.

A: 你能幫我挑選一件晚禮服嗎？

B: 當然可以。

ring sth. up 結帳

A: I want to buy the two suits. Can you ring them up for me?

B: They add up to eight dollars.

A: 我要買這兩套衣服，你能幫我結帳嗎？
B: 它們總共八美元。

return...for a refund 退貨

A: I'm not satisfied with the color of the clothes.

B: You may exchange it but not return it for a refund.

A: 我不滿意這件衣服的顏色。
B: 你可以換一件，但不能退貨。

shop for clothes 買衣服

指逛街買衣服。

A: How often do you shop for clothes?

B: I shop at least twice a week.

A：你多久買一次衣服呢？
B：我一週至少買兩次衣服。

▶▶ Take it or leave it. 別討價還價

A：The shirt is too expensive. I would buy it if you would give me 50% off.

B：Take it or leave it.

A：這件襯衫太貴了，如果你給我對折，我就買了。
B：別討價還價。

▶▶ try on 試穿

A：May I try the suit on?

B：By all means. The fitting room is on the left.

A：我可以試穿這件套裝嗎？
B：當然可以，試衣間在左邊。

02 穿衣服場景

a cap and gown 畢業典禮禮服

方帽與長袍，就是畢業典禮的禮服。

A: The school announced that all students have to dress up for the graduation ceremony.

B: Mary is the only one among us who isn't wearing a cap and gown.

A: 學校宣布，所有學生必須盛裝打扮參加畢業典禮。

B: 瑪麗是我們當中唯一沒有穿畢業典禮禮服的人。

a change of clothes 一套換洗衣服

A: Don't forget to bring a change of clothes with you.

B: What do I wear for the reception?

A: 別忘了帶上你的一套換洗衣服。

B: 我該穿什麼樣的衣服來參加招待會呢？

PART

▶▶ be filled with 充滿

A: The jacket is filled with feathers, so it feels warm to wear.

B: It is perfect for winter wear.

A: 這件夾克充滿羽毛，所以穿起來很溫暖。

B: 冬天穿最合適。

▶▶ bring with 攜帶

A: Please make sure you bring a coat with you because it has been chilly lately.

B: Thanks for reminding me.

A: 請你務必攜帶一件外套，因為最近天氣一直很寒冷。

B: 謝謝你的提醒。

make certain / sure 確定。

change clothes 換衣服

A：I need to change clothes for the party.

B：That's for sure.

A：我需要換衣服參加宴會。

B：那是一定的。

change out of 把…脫下來

A：I slipped on the wet floor.

B：You have to change out of these dirty clothes into something clean.

A：我在溼地板上滑了一跤。

B：你得把這些髒衣服脫下來，換上乾淨的。

come off 掉了

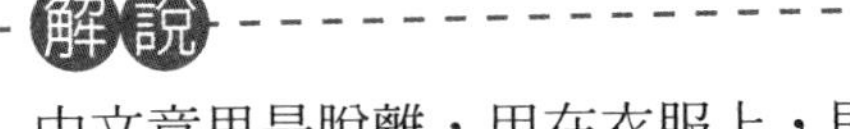

解說

中文意思是脫離，用在衣服上，則指鈕釦掉了。

PART

A: Oh, a button has come off my coat.

B: I can sew it with a needle and thread, and then it'll be as good as new.

A: 啊，我的外套掉了一顆鈕釦。
B: 我可以用針和線來縫合，然後就會完好如新了。

come out 除去

常用來除去汙點、顏色或記號。

A: How do I clean the ink stain on my pants?

B: It shouldn't be a problem. It will come out with detergent and water.

A: 我該如何除去我褲子上的墨水漬？
B: 它應該不是個問題，它用洗衣粉和水就能除去。

do the washing 洗衣服

A: Did you tell your little brother to do the washing?

B: I told him many times.

A: 你有告訴你弟弟要洗衣服嗎？

B: 我告訴他很多次了。

do the washing = do the laundry = wash clothes

fold up 摺疊

A: Would you please fold your clothes up neatly?

B: No problem.

A: 能否請你把你的衣服摺疊整齊呢？

B: 沒問題。

PART

have on 穿上

A: It's really cold today.

B: I know. I had on my coat instead of my T-shirt due to the unusual weather.

A: 今天天氣很涼爽。

B: 我知道，由於天氣異常，所以我必須穿上外套而不是T恤。

hand-me-down 舊衣服

指別人用過的舊東西，特別指家中的大哥、大姊傳給小弟、小妹穿的衣服。

A: I am tired of getting hand-me-downs.

B: That's what happens when you are the younger child in the family.

A: 我厭倦拿到舊衣服。

B: 當你是家裡年幼的孩子時，這種事情就會發生。

take off 脫下

A：Aren't you hot? Why are you wearing a jacket? You should take it off.

B：No, I'm fine. Thanks.

A：你不熱嗎？你為什麼穿著一件夾克呢？你應該脫下來。

B：不，我不熱，謝謝。

evening dress 晚禮服

A：What should you wear for the reception tonight?

B：I'll be wearing my new evening dress, which I bought specifically.

A：今晚你該穿什麼去參加招待會？

B：我會穿我特別買的新晚禮服。

PART

hang up 掛起來

A：Go and hang the washing out to dry.

B：Ok, I'll hang them up on the washing line.

A：去把洗好的衣服掛出去晒乾。

B：好的，我會掛在洗衣繩上。

Make yourself at home. 請不要客氣

請把這兒當做是你家，暗示無拘無束與隨意，引申爲請不要客氣。

A：Do you mind if I take off my coat?

B：Make yourself at home.

A：你介意我脫下外套嗎？

B：請不要客氣。

pack away 收藏

A：Winter is finally over and spring is here.

B：Soon it will be time to pack our winter clothes away.

A：冬天終於結束了，春天來了。

B：很快地收藏冬天衣服的時間到了。

put on 穿上

此片語是強調穿的動作。

A：It's freezing outside.

B：Better put on a jacket if you go out tonight.

A：外面好冷。

B：如果你今晚外出，最好穿上一件夾克。

sell like hot cakes 銷售得很快

A：What will they put on a show for?

B：They hope their clothes sell like hot cakes.

A：他們為什麼要演戲呢？

B：他們希望他們的衣服銷售得很快。

sew up 縫合

A：I asked Susan to sew up the hole in my coat.

B：She is a nice person who always helps her friends.

A：我要求蘇珊縫合我大衣上的破洞。

B：她人很好，經常幫助朋友。

slip sb.'s mind 忘記

slip 忘記或未注意到。

A: Did you pick up my clothes from the laundry?

B: Oh, sorry. It slipped my mind.

A: 你有去洗衣店拿我的衣服嗎？
B: 哦，對不起，我忘了。

補充

slip sb.'s mind = slip sb.'s memory

▶▶ Sunday best 最漂亮的衣服

A: You look like you put on your Sunday best.

B: Because I will go to church later.

A: 你似乎穿了你最漂亮的衣服。
B: 因為待會兒我要去做禮拜。

補充

Sunday best = Sunday (best) clothes = glad clothes

▶▶ wash out 洗掉

A: I've washed this white shirt twice, but the ink stain still hasn't completely been washed out.

B: You can send it over to the dry cleaner's.

A: 這件白色襯衣我已洗兩遍了，但上面的墨水漬還是無法完全洗掉。

B: 你可以把它送去乾洗店。

wash out = come out = come off

▶▶ wear layers of clothes 穿多層次衣服

A: I don't like wearing layers of clothes in winter.

B: Me too. That makes me look like a big snowball.

A: 在冬天裡，我不喜歡穿多層次衣服。

B: 我也一樣，那樣會讓我看起來像是大雪球。

wear out 穿破

A: Why don't you wear the light blue pants?

B: I love those pants, but they're a bit worn out.

A: 你為什麼不穿這條淺藍色褲子呢？

B: 我喜歡這條褲子，但是這條褲子有點破了。

PART

03 衣服評價場景

▶▶ a second opinion 其他人的意見

A: What do you think of this sweater?

B: Well, I think it is ok, but you should get a second opinion.

A: 你認為這件毛衣怎麼樣呢？

B: 嗯，我想它還好，但是你應該聽其他人的意見。

類似片語有 second thought 重新考慮。

▶▶ catch on 流行

catch on 當流行使用時，主詞必須是物。

A: The style of clothes is pretty cool and I think it will catch on quickly.

B: That's for sure.

A：這個款式的衣服很漂亮，我想它一定會很快流行起來的。

B：那是一定的。

dress up 盛裝打扮

A：Betty dressed up for the reception last night.

B：Yeah, she looked so nice.

A：昨晚貝蒂盛裝打扮參加招待會。

B：是啊，她看起來好美。

dress down 穿著隨便

比平時穿的還隨便，爲因應某些場合而必須穿得樸素。

A：I dressed down for my birthday party today.

B：It's better to dress up than dress down.

A：今天我穿著隨便地參加我的生日宴會。

B：盛裝打扮比穿著隨便要好。

dressed to kill 打扮很迷人

A：Look, Lorna was dressed to kill.

B：She was in the spot-light at the reception because she was wearing her best clothes.

A：瞧，蘿拉打扮得很迷人。

B：她是招待會的焦點，因為她穿上她最好的衣服。

in fashion 流行

A：What's in at the moment?

B：This kind of dress is now in fashion.

A：現在流行什麼呢？

B：這種款式的女裝現在很流行。

▶▶ in style 時髦

指流行。

A: Do you think my clothes are in style?

B: Actually, I haven't seen that style of clothes in a long time.

A: 你認為我的衣服很時髦嗎？

B: 事實上，我很久沒看到這種款式的衣服了。

▶▶ in vogue 流行

A: This kind of dress is now in vogue.

B: But it was not in fashion last year.

A: 這款衣服現在很流行。

B: 但是它去年並不流行。

nice-looking 漂亮的

A: That is really a nice-looking jacket. It must have cost you a fortune.

B: You are asking the wrong person. I borrowed it from Betty.

A: 那是一件很漂亮的夾克，它一定花了你好多錢。

B: 你問錯人了，這是我從貝蒂那裡借的。

nice-looking = good-looking = great-looking = best-looking = decent-looking

out of date 過時的

A: Why do you always read "Vogue" magazine?

B: It shows me which styles are out of date and which styles are current fashionable trends.

A: 你為什麼總是閱讀「時尚」雜誌呢？

B: 它告訴我哪些款式是過時的、哪些款式是目前的流行趨勢。

out of style 過時

指不流行；style 是指流行的樣式。

A: What do you think about this suit?

B: Honestly, it looks out of style.

A: 你認為這套衣服怎麼樣？

B: 老實說，它看起來過時了。

in order 整整齊齊的

強調井然有序。

A: Have you packed your suitcase?

B: Yes, everything is in order now.

A: 你已經整理好衣箱了嗎？

B: 整理好了，現在每件都是整整齊齊的。

補充

(1) in order 按照順序，I informed my classmates in order that the field trip will be cancelled. 我按照順序通知我的同學，戶外教學將被取消。

(2) in order 合適的，Wearing leisure clothes in the picnic is in order. 在野餐中，穿休閒服是合適的。

PART 

第 3 單元

住生活片語

01 睡覺場景

02 住宿場景

03 相處場景

04 布置場景

05 住的評價

06 電話場景

07 電視場景

08 電腦場景

09 網路場景

10 印表機與影印機場景

11 電器故障場景

12 其他住場景

PART

01 睡覺場景

be off to bed 上床睡覺

A: Knock off the noise. I'll be off to bed.

B: Sorry to have disturbed you.

A: 不許再出聲，我要上床睡覺了。

B: 對不起，吵到你了。

be wide awake 無法入睡

指很清醒。

A: Are you ready to go to sleep?

B: No, I had too much caffeine and am wide awake.

A: 你準備好去睡覺了嗎？

B: 沒有，我喝了太多咖啡因，因而無法入睡。

catch up on 補充

A: After the work, I need to catch up on some sleep.

B: Me, too. Now I am tired.

A: 工作完後，我需要補充睡眠。

B: 我也是，現在我很累。

count sheep 數羊

心裡計算羊數以求入睡。

A: I am having a hard time going to sleep.

B: Why don’t you try counting sheep?

A: 我睡不著覺。

B: 你為什麼不試著數羊來入睡呢？

dead to the world 睡得很沉

A: Michelle has been studying for her finals all night.

B: Yeah, I tried to talk to her but she is dead to the world right now.

A: 米雪兒為了期末考讀了一整夜的書。

B: 沒錯，我想和她說話，但是她現在睡得很沉。

doze off 打瞌睡

A: Everybody dozes off in his class.

B: Me, too. I must drink at least two cups of coffee to stay awake in his class.

A: 上他的課，每一個人都會打瞌睡。

B: 我也是，上他的課，我至少要喝兩杯咖啡來保持清醒。

early riser 早起者

A：I heard you were often late for morning classes this semester.

B：Yeah, I am not much of an early riser.

A：我聽說你這學期早上的課常遲到。

B：沒錯，我不是早起者。

補充

early bird = morning person

feel drowsy 想睡覺

A：I feel drowsy after lunch.

B：You must have eaten too much.

A：午餐後，我就想睡覺。

B：你一定吃太多了。

PART

get to sleep 睡著

A: I couldn't sleep last night.

B: If you turn over, you might find it easier to get to sleep.

A: 我昨晚失眠。

B: 如果你翻翻身，就會更容易睡著。

have a late night 晚點睡

A: I'll have a late night tonight.

B: Going to sleep early is good for your health.

A: 今晚我要晚點睡。

B: 早點睡有利於你的健康。

have an early night 早點睡

A: Would you like to go and see a movie?

B: I'd love to, but I think I'll have an early night.

A：你想要去看電影嗎？
B：我很想去看，但是我想我要早點睡。

drop off to sleep 睡著

A：I haven't been able to drop off to sleep lately.

B：Maybe exercising in the evening will help you get to sleep.

A：我最近都睡不著。
B：或許在晚上做做運動能幫助你入睡。

fall asleep 睡著

A：What did you think of the movie?

B：I thought it was very boring and very stupid. I had to try really hard not to fall asleep.

A：你覺得這部電影怎麼樣？
B：我認為這部電影很無聊且乏味，我必須硬撐著不睡著。

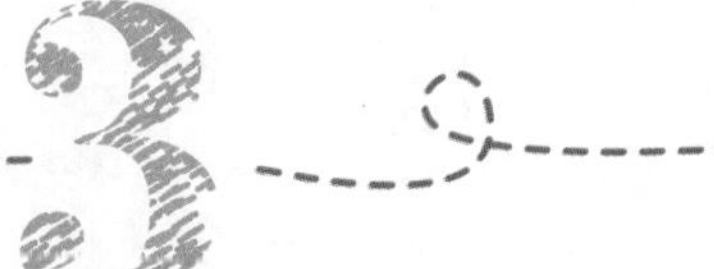

go to bed with the lamb and rise with the lark 早睡早起

直譯是「隨小羊上床，隨百靈鳥起床」，引申為早睡早起。

A：For a healthy body, I go to bed with the lamb and rise with the lark every day.

B：That's right. I can't help thinking the same.

A：為了身體健康，我每天都早睡早起。
B：那很對，我也有同樣的想法。

head off for bed 去睡覺

A：It's getting on for midnight. It is time to head off for bed.

B：But I have not finished writing my homework.

A：快到午夜了，睡覺的時間到了。
B：但是我還沒寫完我的回家作業。

hit the sack 睡覺

A：It's time to hit the sack.

B：Yeah, you look very tired.

A：該睡覺時間到了。

B：沒錯，你看起來非常累。

hit the hay 睡覺

A：Why do you always drink a glass of milk before hitting the hay?

B：It helps me get a better night's sleep.

A：你為什麼總是在睡覺前喝一杯牛奶呢？

B：它幫助我一夜好眠。

hit the hay = hit the stack

PART

nod off 打瞌睡

A: Today, I saw you were nodding off during math class. What happened?

B: I couldn't sleep last night, so I was exhausted today.

A: 今天我看見你在數學課打瞌睡，發生什麼事情了嗎？

B: 我昨晚無法入睡，因此今天很疲倦。

sleep a wink 睡覺

此片語用在否定句，指睡一會兒或打個盹兒的意思。

A: I didn't sleep a wink with those dogs barking all night long.

B: No wonder you are so grumpy.

A: 我整晚因為狗叫聲而沒睡覺。

B: 難怪你如此生氣。

sleep in 睡過頭

A：I just want to sleep in this morning until I feel like getting up.

B：Then you will sleep in and miss the bus.

A：今天早晨我只想睡覺，直到睡夠了再起床。

B：那麼你會因為睡過頭而沒趕上公車。

sleeping pill 安眠藥

A：What are those pills you are taking?

B：I'm taking sleeping pills to help with my insomnia.

A：你在吃的那些藥是什麼？

B：我正在吃安眠藥來治療我的失眠症。

PART

take a nap 小睡一下

指小睡一會兒或睡午覺。

A: I got up early today and now I am a little tired.

B: You had better find somewhere to take a nap.

A: 我今天起得很早，而現在我有點累。

B: 你最好找地方來小睡一下。

toss and turn 輾轉反側

身體輾轉反側，通常表示難以入睡。

A: I couldn't sleep last night. All I did was toss and turn.

B: Did you try taking any sleeping pills?

A: 我昨晚失眠，整晚輾轉反側。

B: 你有吃安眠藥嗎？

turn in 上床睡覺

A：I'm tired. I guess it is time for me to turn in.

B：As the old saying goes, "don't put off until tomorrow what can be done today".

A：我累了，我想我該上床睡覺時間到了。

B：就像古老的諺語所說的：「今日事今日畢」。

PART

02 住宿場景

adapt oneself to 適應

A: Does going away to school for the first time make you nervous?

B: I guess so. I just need time to adapt myself to a new place.

A: 第一次離家上學，會讓你感覺緊張嗎？

B: 會啊，我只是需要時間去適應新的環境。

against keeping pets 禁止養寵物

A: Does the apartment have rules against keeping pets?

B: Yes, we don't like the noise or smell from animals, so we prohibit it.

A: 這間公寓有規定禁止養寵物嗎？

B: 有啊，我們不喜歡動物的噪音和氣味，所以禁止養寵物。

be stuck with sb. 被迫跟某人在一起

A：I heard Abel will move into your apartment. Is it for sure?

B：You bet. I will be stuck with him for six months.

A：我聽說亞伯要搬進你的公寓，確定了嗎？

B：確定了，我被迫跟他在一起住六個月。

back and forth 來回地

A：I am sick of going back and forth to school this semester.

B：Could you move into the dorm? The rooms are nice, but it's a little expensive.

A：我厭倦在這個學期來回奔波地上下學。

B：你可以搬進宿舍嗎？房間很好，不過價格有一點貴。

PART

find an apartment 找房子

A: What are you doing?

B: I was surfing the net to find an apartment.

A: 你現在在做什麼？

B: 我在上網找房子。

find an apartment = look for a house

fully booked 客滿

A: I am traveling to Taipei this weekend and haven't yet made a hotel reservation.

B: You'd better hurry. This is a holiday weekend and the hotels are likely to be fully booked.

A: 我這個週末會去臺北旅行，還沒有預訂旅館。

B: 你最好快一點，這個週末是假日週末，旅館很可能全部客滿了。

fully booked = full up = full ；make a reservation 預訂；confirm a reservation 確認預訂；cancel a reservation 取消預訂。

get possession of 擁有

A：I have got possession of the house for three years.

B：After years of saving, I should be able to afford one.

A：我已擁有那房子3年了。

B：經過數年儲蓄後，我應該能夠買一棟。

get used to 習慣於

A：We are moving to Arizona in the middle of the desert.

B：It's going to be very hot there. You are going to have a tough time getting used to the weather.

A：我們要搬到沙漠中央的亞利桑納州。

B：那裡的天氣將會很熱，你要適應天氣會有困難。

PART

live on campus 住校

A: Do all freshmen have to live on campus?

B: No, they may choose freely to live on or off campus.

A: 所有一年級新生都必須住校嗎？

B: 不，他們可以自由選擇住校或住校外。

look for a needle in a hay stack 大海撈針

A: I am trying to find a cheap but nice place to live.

B: That will be like looking for a needle in a hay stack.

A: 我正試著找一間便宜又舒適的住所居住。

B: 那可能會像大海撈針一樣。

move out 搬出

A: I heard you and Joe are thinking of moving out of the campus to a new place.

B: Yes. I prefer living off campus.

A: 我聽說你和喬正想搬出校園到一個新的住所。

B: 沒錯，我比較喜歡住在校外。

moving sale 遷移拍賣

A: I'm going to move into the dorm next weekend. But I won't have enough space to fit all of my furniture.

B: Why don't you have a moving sale to get rid of everything you can't take along?

A: 我下週末要搬進宿舍，但是我沒有足夠的空間來放我所有的家具。

B: 你為什麼不舉辦一個遷移拍賣來清掉你不能帶走的東西呢？

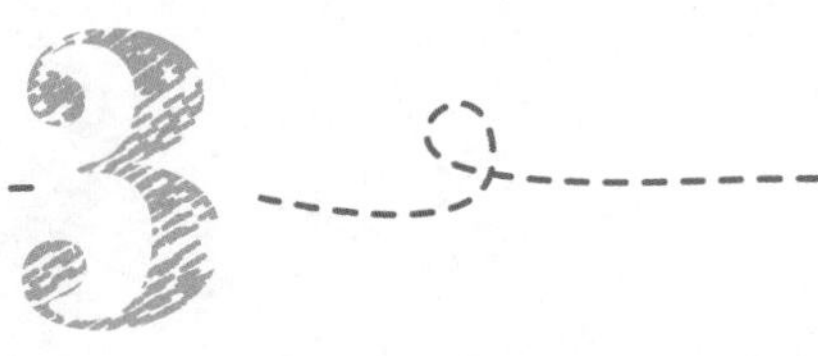

on the other side 另外一邊

A: Can you give me a lift to the business center?

B: I'd like to, but I live on the other side of town.

A: 你能讓我搭便車到商業中心嗎？

B: 我很樂意，但是我居住在城市的另外一邊。

put up 提供食宿

A: Alice has a heart of gold and often helps others without asking for any reward.

B: I think so, too. She put me up for a few days while I was visiting Boston.

A: 愛麗絲心地很好，常不求回報地幫助別人。

B: 我也這麼覺得，上次我去波士頓拜訪時，她提供了我幾天的食宿。

rent money 租金

A：My landlord needs the rent money. He is beginning to lose patience with me.

B：You had better pay it before you get evicted.

A：我的房東需要租金，他開始對我失去耐性。

B：在你被逐出之前，最好付房租。

ride out 安全度過

A：I think we should stay home and ride out the storm.

B：I agree. We can never be too careful.

A：我想我們應該待在家裡以安全度過暴風雨。

B：我同意，我們越小心越好。

PART

room and board 食宿費

A: The cost of room and board is going up next semester.

B: This happens every semester.

A: 食宿費下學期會上漲。
B: 每一學期都會發生這種事情。

sign the contract 簽契約

A: I've signed the contract with the landlord on my own.

B: Do you think you can afford it?

A: 我已經跟房東簽了契約。
B: 你認為你付得起它嗎？

stay at 暫住

指短暫的停留或投宿在某地。

A：Which hotel will you be staying at?

B：I'm lodging at the Grand Hotel.

A：你會暫住在哪一間旅館呢？

B：我會暫住在圓山大飯店。

stay at = lodge at

stay over 過夜

A：That's too bad that I missed the last train.

B：Why don't you just stay over at my house?

A：太糟糕了，我沒趕上末班火車。

B：你為什麼不在我家過夜呢？

stay over = sleep over = stay the night

▶▶ tear down 拆毀

A: If the dormitory is in bad shape, it ought to be torn down.

B: I couldn't agree with you more.

A: 如果宿舍狀況不好，就應該被拆除。

B: 我非常同意。

▶▶ walk-in 無預約

指未經預訂的散客。

A: Do you take any walk-in guests?

B: I'd like to, but our hotel has no vacancy.

A：你接不接受無預約的客人？

B：我很願意接受，但是我們的旅館客滿了。

walk-up 無電梯的

A：I need a nice place within a thirty-minute walk to work.

B：You can try to look for a low-rise walk-up apartment on the web.

A：我需要一個好的住所，走路上班不要超過30分鐘。

B：你可以在網路上尋找層數少而無電梯的公寓。

03 相處場景

a man of few words 沉默寡言的人

A: What do you think of your roommate?

B: He is a man of few words.

A: 你認為你的室友怎麼樣？
B: 他是個沉默寡言的人。

agree like cats and dogs 完全合不來

像貓和狗一樣合不來。

A: How are you getting along with your roommate?

B: We agree like cats and dogs.

A: 你跟你的室友相處得怎麼樣呢？
B: 我們完全合不來。

be critical of 不滿意

指不滿、挑剔或批評。

A：The professor is very critical of new students.

B：Maybe they are newcomers, so they don't know the rules.

A：這位教授對新學生非常不滿意。
B：或許他們是新來的，所以他們不懂規則。

be not good with sb. 和某人相處不好

A：Can you baby-sit for me tonight?

B：I'm really sorry, but I am not good with kids.

A：你今晚能幫我照顧小孩嗎？
B：我真的很抱歉，我和小孩處不來。

be on terms with sb. 友好

指關係良好。

A：I need a new roommate who is neat and considerate.

B：You mean to say you're not on good terms with your former roommate.

A：我需要一個愛整潔和體貼的新室友。

B：你意思是說你跟你的前任室友處得不好。

busy-body 愛說閒話的人

A：Fiona is a busy-body by nature.

B：I know. I will never tell her any of my secrets.

A：費歐娜生性是個愛說閒話的人。

B：我知道，我絕不會告訴她我的任何一個祕密。

buy sb.'s story 相信某人的話

A: Scott said he missed school because he was sick.

B: I don't buy your story. I think he went to the beach.

A: 史考特說，他沒上學，因為他病了。

B: 我不相信你的話，我想他去了海灘。

check with sb. 問過

指跟某人聯繫或商量。

A: Do you know anyone who can watch my cat tomorrow?

B: Have you checked with Judy?

A: 你知道有誰明天能照顧我的貓嗎？

B: 你有問過茱蒂嗎？

clear the air 消除誤會

A：I don't like my roommate. She is very selfish.

B：You should have a chat with her and clear the air between the two of you.

A：我不喜歡我的室友，她非常自私。

B：你應該跟她聊一聊，消除你們倆之間的誤會。

cold shoulder 冷淡

與the連用，動詞常用give或get。

A：Why have you been giving me the cold shoulder lately?

B：Because I didn't appreciate what you said about me.

A：你為什麼最近一直對我很冷淡呢？

B：因為我不喜歡你說的那些關於我的話。

find sb.'s feet 適應新環境

A: I just moved and I cannot seem to find my feet.

B: New York is a big place, and will take some time to get used to.

A: 我剛搬來，似乎不能適應新環境。

B: 紐約是個大城市，需要一段時間才能適應。

fit into 適應

強調相處融洽。

A: I hope I can fit into the new school.

B: I am sure you will make some friends there.

A: 我希望我能適應新學校。

B: 我確信你會在當地交到一些朋友。

補充

fit into = fit in

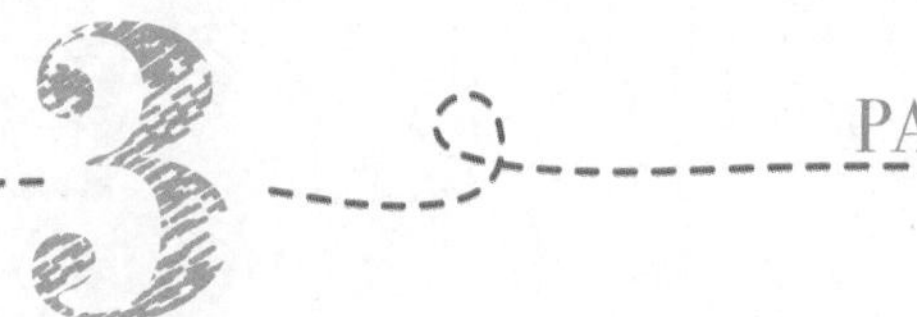

PART

hit it off 合得來

強調一開始就相處很好。

A: Unfortunately, I didn't really hit it off with my roommate.

B: You are under a 6-month lease, so you should try to make it work.

A: 不幸的是，我和我的室友並不很合得來。

B: 你的租期尚有六個月，所以你應該設法重新合好。

get along with sb. 與某人相處

A: I don't get along with Mary that well.

B: Me, neither. It seems like we disagree about everything.

A: 我沒有跟瑪麗相處得很好。

B: 我也是，我們似乎經常爭論不休。

get on with sb. 與某人相處

處在和睦關係之中。

A：Amanda is on my mind. Do you know her new phone number?

B：Sorry. I didn't get on with her when she left.

A：我想念艾曼達，你知道她的新電話號碼嗎？
B：對不起，她離開時，我與她處得並不好。

make peace with sb. 跟某人和好

A：Have you made peace with your roommate yet?

B：Not yet, he hasn't accepted my apology.

A：你有跟你室友和好了嗎？
B：還沒有，他還沒有接受我的道歉。

補充

make peace with sb. = live peace with sb.

PART

out of place 不自在

A: I feel out of place at this school.

B: Well, private schools are more formal than public ones.

A: 在這所學校裡，我感到不自在。

B: 嗯，私人學校比公立學校更加注重社交禮儀。

out of place 有「不應該」的意思，如 It's out of place to make noise at night. 晚上製造噪音很不應該。

put up with 忍受

A: My roommate has to repeat a year.

B: You mean you have to put up with her for another whole year.

A: 我的室友必須留級一年。

B: 你是說你必須再忍受她一整年。

▶▶ rotten to the core 糟透

直譯爲「腐爛到核心」，指壞透了或爛透了。

A：What happened to Jeff and Frank?

B：Not sure, but their friendship is now rotten to the core.

A：傑夫和法蘭克發生了什麼事？

B：不清楚，但是他們的友誼現在糟透了。

▶▶ rub elbows with sb. 與某人交往

A：I like to attend the parties because it gives me the chance to rub elbows with the stars.

B：No wonder, you know many famous people.

A：我喜歡參加宴會，因為它給了我與明星交往的機會。

B：難怪，你認識許多名人。

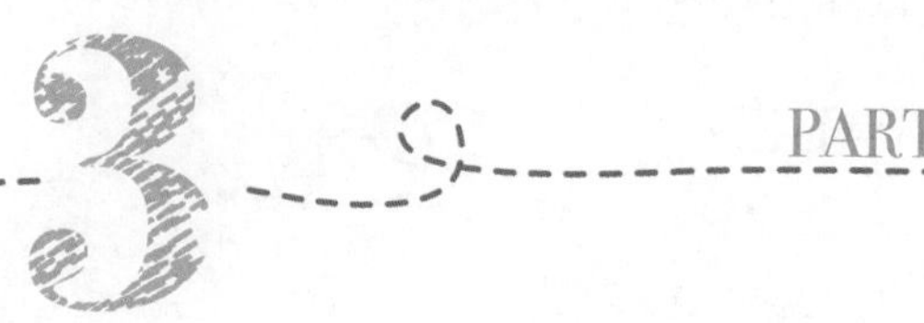

sour grapes 酸葡萄心態

A：I am envious of their relationship.

B：Sounds like sour grapes.

A：我嫉妒他們的關係。
B：聽起來像是酸葡萄心態。

take into account 考慮

A：I'm going to invite my friends to go to a club tonight.

B：You have to take into account that Jim and Eric are not getting along right now.

A：今晚我會邀請我的朋友去一個俱樂部玩玩。
B：你必須要考慮到吉姆和艾利克現在並沒有處得很好。

through the grapevine 間接地

指小道消息。

A: I learned through the grapevine that you don't like your roommate.

B: You shouldn't listen to gossip. We are getting along well.

A: 我間接得知你不喜歡你的室友。

B: 你不該聽信謠言，我們相處得很好。

04 布置場景

▶▶ clean up 打掃乾淨

強調清潔整齊與有秩序。

A：Do me a favor and clean up the room, will you?

B：Sure, as long as you agree to clean it next time.

A：幫忙我把房間打掃乾淨，好嗎？

B：當然可以，只要你願意下次把房間打掃乾淨就好了。

▶▶ decorate with 用…裝飾

A：The teacher said that Taiwanese often decorate their houses with red ornaments.

B：That's because the color red symbolizes luck.

A：老師說臺灣人常用紅色裝飾品來裝飾房子。

B：那是因為紅色代表吉祥。

fill the bill 符合要求

A: I'm looking for some used furniture which is not too expensive.

B: I know one place that could fill the bill for you.

A: 我正在找一些便宜的二手家具。

B: 我知道有一個地方，能符合你的要求。

fit up 裝飾

指把東西放置好或裝備一些附屬必需品。

A: I'll fit up the house with the window glass.

B: It will cost you a lot of money.

A: 我會用窗玻璃來裝飾房子。

B: 那將會花掉你很多錢。

pick up 收拾

A: Look at the mess you made in the living room.

B: I will pick up the living room when I finish my homework.

A: 看看你把客廳弄得一團糟。

B: 當我做完家庭作業後，我就會收拾客廳。

put away 收拾

A: Make sure you put away your toys before going to bed.

B: Ok, I'll do it right now.

A: 你在睡覺前一定要將你的玩具收拾好。

B: 好的，我馬上就做這件事。

straighten up 整理

A: Your room is a real dump.

B：I know I need to straighten it up.

A：你的房間真是又髒又亂。
B：我知道我需要把房間整理一下。

tidy up 收拾

把混亂的場面，整理得井然有序。

A：Could you lend me a hand to paint the house?

B：Sure. But I want to tidy up my room first.

A：你能幫我粉刷房子嗎？
B：當然可以，但我想先把我的房間收拾一下。

mess up 弄髒

A：The rest rooms are really messed up because they don't have soap or paper towels.

B：Awful. I think you should tell the manager.

A：這廁所弄得很髒，因為沒有肥皂或紙巾。

B：真可怕，我想你應該告訴經理。

take out the garbage 倒垃圾

A：Could you take out the garbage for me right now?

B：I am busy fixing the sink.

A：你現在能幫我倒垃圾嗎？

B：我正忙著修理水槽。

take out 拿出去。

05 住的評價

as silent as the grave 非常安靜

像墳墓一樣的安靜。

A: I'm an auditory learner and I need to find a quiet place to study.

B: The private rooms at the library are always as silent as the grave.

A: 我是一個聽覺型學習者，我需要找一個安靜的地方讀書。

B: 在圖書館的私人房間總是非常安靜。

at sixes and sevens 亂七八糟的

A: I can't find your note now.

B: Everything in my room is at sixes and sevens after taking the finals.

A：我現在找不到你的筆記本。

B：期末考後，我房間裡的每樣東西都亂七八糟的。

be better off 生活更好

指生活更舒適或者指所處的情境好轉起來。

A：The apartment looks fantastic.

B：You'll be better off staying there since it is so close to the campus.

A：這間公寓看起來真不錯。

B：你住在那裡生活會更好，因為它離校園很近。

be satisfied with 對…滿意

A：I was satisfied with the adornment of the room.

B：I think it must cost you a fortune.

A：我對房間布置很滿意。
B：我想它一定花了你不少錢。

hustle and bustle 喧鬧忙亂

A：Taipei is a hustle and bustle city.

B：Fortunately, I live far away from the downtown area.

A：臺北是一個喧鬧忙亂的城市。
B：幸運的是，我住的地方離市區很遠。

in a mess 亂糟糟

形容一片混亂與骯髒。

A：Can we study at your home instead?

B：Why? Is your room in a mess?

A：我們可以改在你家讀書嗎？
B：為什麼？因為你房間亂糟糟的嗎？

neat and tidy 乾淨整潔

A: I found the room is neat and tidy.

B: Mercy cleaned the room this morning.

A：我發現這間房間乾淨整潔。
B：今天早上梅西打掃了這間房間。

nothing like 什麼都比不上

A: The cold is more than I can bear.

B: There's nothing like staying in a warm home.

A：寒冷超過我忍受的程度。
B：什麼都比不上待在溫暖的房間裡好。

pros and cons 優缺點

A: Do you live on or off campus?

B: Well, I'm thinking about the pros and cons of both options.

A: 你要住校內或校外呢？

B: 嗯，我在考慮兩者的優缺點。

spick-and-span 乾淨

形容某物非常整齊清潔與無斑點。

A: Your apartment always looks great. It's so spotless and neat.

B: I'm always trying to keep it spick-and-span.

A: 你的公寓隨時看起來都很不錯，一塵不染又很整潔。

B: 我隨時都保持它的乾淨。

spruce up 裝修

爲某物打扮整齊，使之變得更漂亮。

A: The house is in an excellent location but it looks a little old.

B: It just needs to spruce up of a bit.

A: 這間房子地點很好，但是看起來有點舊。

B: 它只需要稍微裝修一下。

topsy-turvy 亂七八糟的

處於無秩序與混亂的狀態。

A: I can't believe your room is topsy-turvy.

B: That's not my room. My room is the opposite room.

A: 我無法相信你的房間亂七八糟的。

B: 那不是我的房間，我的房間在對面。

06 電話場景

a phone call away
打個電話就過來幫忙的人

A: I can't go to the student center. I'm working on my lab report.

B: If you need my help, please let me know. I'm only a phone call away.

A: 我不能去學生活動中心，我正在寫我的實驗報告。

B: 如果你需要我的幫忙，請讓我知道。只要打個電話，我就會來幫忙。

accept the charge 付錢

A: There is a collect call from a man named Andy. Will you accept the charge?

B: No, I don't know anyone named Andy.

A: 有一通付費電話來自名叫安迪的男人，你要付錢嗎？

B: 不，我不認識叫什麼安迪的人。

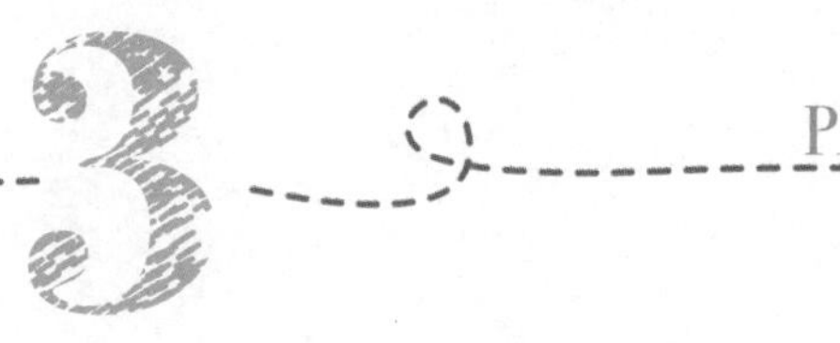

be sick of 討厭

指感到厭倦或厭惡。

A: I'm sick of calling the landlord to complain about the faucet leaking.

B: As it happens, I called her this morning.

A: 我很討厭打電話給房東抱怨水龍頭漏水。
B: 剛好，我今天早上已經打電話給她了。

call around 打電話詢問

A: Could you tell me Mary's e-mail address?

B: I'm not sure, but you'd better call around.

A: 你能告訴我瑪麗的電子郵件地址嗎？
B: 我不確定，但是你最好打電話詢問。

call back 回電話

A: I guess I should try to call back.

B: Yes. He'd probably give you a hand.

A: 我想我該設法回電話。

B: 沒錯，他很可能會幫你一把。

call in sick 打電話請病假

A: Why didn't I see Alice this morning?

B: She felt uncomfortable, so she called in sick.

A: 今天早上我為什麼沒看到愛麗絲呢？

B: 她覺得不舒服，所以她打電話請病假。

collect call 受話方付費

A: You have an overseas collect call from Mr. Vincent in California.

B: I will accept the charges.

A：你有一通來自加州的文森先生的受話方付費國際電話。

B：我接受付費。

▶▶ cut down on 減少

只在價格或數量上的減少。

A：My phone bill this month is too high.

B：I think you should try to cut down on calling your girlfriend abroad.

A：這個月我的電話帳單太貴了。

B：我想你應該減少打電話給你的國外女朋友。

▶▶ cutting-edge 先進

指尖端或前衛。

A：I see your cell phone is cutting-edge.

B：You said it. It can take pictures, not to mention it can receive voice mail, and text messages.

A：我知道你的手機很先進。

B：你說對了，它除了可以照相，更不用說還可以接收語音郵件和簡訊。

▶▶ get off the phone 掛上電話

A：Andrew, get off the phone. I am expecting a call.

B：Give me five minutes, please.

A：安德魯，把電話掛上，我正在等電話。

B：請再給我五分鐘時間。

▶▶ give sb. a call 給某人打電話

A：Let's have dinner together sometime.

B：Sounds good. Give me a call, please.

A：改天我們一起吃晚餐吧。
B：聽起來不錯，請打電話給我。

charge up 充電

A: My cell phone battery is dead; it needs recharging.

B: You can charge up your cell phone over there.

A：我的手機電池沒電了，需要充電。
B：你可以在那邊給你的手機充電。

give out 外流

指透露或公開訊息。

A: May I have your phone number, please?

B: Actually, I am not allowed to give out my phone number.

A：我可以有你的電話號碼嗎？

B：事實上，我不允許我的電話號碼外流。

hold on 不掛斷電話

在電話場景中，指不掛斷電話。

A：I have another call. Can you hold on?

B：Sure, but this is a long distance call, so please don't talk too long.

A：我有電話插播，你能不掛斷電話嗎？

B：可以，但是這是長途電話，所以請你不要講太久。

hold on = hold up；hang up = get off 掛斷電話。

leave a message 留言

A：Did you inform her that her appointment has

been cancelled?

B: I left a message on her voice mail.

A: 你有通知她取消約會嗎？

B: 我有在她的語音信箱留言。

比較 take a message 與 leave a message 差別，take a message 是幫助別人留言，而 leave a message 是留言，如 May l take a message for you? 我可以幫你留言嗎？May you leave a message? 你可以留言嗎？

long distance 長途電話

A: Look at the incredible long distance bill. Do you think we can afford that every month?

B: Don't worry. As of today, I'm going to contact my girlfriend by e-mail.

A: 看看這驚人的長途電話費，你認為我們每個月可以負擔得起嗎？

B: 不要擔心，從今天起，我會用電子郵件跟我女友聯絡。

loose change 零錢

A: I need 50 cents for the payphone.

B: Sorry, I don't have any loose change to give you.

A: 我需要50分錢打公共電話。

B: 對不起，我沒有任何零錢可以給你。

out of the blue 突然地

用在沒有想到或未預測到的情況下。

A: Mike called me totally out of the blue yesterday.

B: Wow, I haven't talked to him in years.

A: 昨天麥克突然打電話給我。

B: 哇，我好多年沒有跟他談話了。

pay phone 付費公用電話

A: Excuse me. Do you know where the nearest pay phone is?

B: Well, the nearest one is at the student dorm.

A: 打擾一下，你知道最近的付費公用電話在何處嗎？

B: 嗯，最近的付費公用電話是在學生宿舍。

put through 轉接電話

A: May I speak to Mr. Brown?

B: Just a second. I'll put you through.

A: 我想找布朗先生？

B: 等一下，我會幫你轉接電話。

run up to 達到

run up to 後面接數字，意思爲「達到」；而 run up to 後面接地點，意思爲「匆忙去」的意思。

A：My phone bill ran up to $1,000 this month.

B：You'd better start calling less.

A：這個月，我的電話帳單達到1,000美元。

B：你最好開始少打電話。

PART

07 電視場景

be obsessed with 沉迷於

A: Mike is obsessed with watching TV.

B: I hope he can try to find something useful to do.

A: 麥可沉迷於看電視。

B: 我希望他能盡量找些有用的事來做。

be obsessed with = be obsessed by

come on 上演

A: When is the show going to come on?

B: It starts at 10 o'clock every night.

A: 這個節目何時上演呢？

B: 每晚10點開始。

change the channel 轉台

指調換電視頻道。

A: Can you change the channel for me? I want to see the weather.

B: Ok, I'll change to channel 2.

A: 你可以幫我轉台嗎？我想要看天氣預報。

B: 可以，我會轉到第二頻道去。

couch potato 電視迷

直譯爲「沙發馬鈴薯」，指花很多時間坐著或躺著，表示懶散或懶蟲，尤其是指花很多時間在看電視。

A: As it is, I can hardly get along without watching TV every day.

B: You are really a couch potato. You should get out more.

A：事實上，我每天沒有看電視會很難過。

B：你真是一個電視迷，你應該多出去走走。

keep down 降低

A: It's nearly midnight. Could you keep the noise level down?

B: All right. I'll turn the volume down on the TV straight away.

A：接近午夜了，你能降低音量嗎？

B：可以，我立刻把電視音量轉小聲。

leave on 留在

A: Why don't you stop channel surfing and just leave it on the Discovery channel?

B: Because I am not interested in watching how whales live.

A：你為什麼不停地轉台，就留在探索頻道吧？

B：因為我沒興趣看鯨魚如何生活。

switch off 關閉

指關掉電燈或電視等電器。

A：Please switch off the TV. I'm studying my American Literature.

B：Can you study in another room? I am watching my favorite TV show.

A：請你關閉電視，我正在研讀美國文學。

B：你能去別的房間讀書嗎？我正在看我最喜歡的電視節目。

tune in 收看

A：My television is broken. I can't tune in to my favorite channel.

B：You should bring your TV to the repair shop.

A：我的電視壞了，我不能收看我最喜歡的頻道。

B：你應該帶你的電視去維修店。

turn down 調低

A: The TV is too loud and I am trying to attend to my work.

B: I'm sorry. I will turn down the volume.

A: 電視太吵了，而我正專心地工作。

B: 抱歉，我會調低音量。

turn off 關掉

A: Let's turn off the TV and go for a walk.

B: I know I need to stop being such a couch potato.

A: 我們關掉電視去散步吧。

B: 我知道，我要停止當一個電視迷。

go for a walk 散步。

wear and tear 磨損

指經過時間歲月而耗損。

A: What's wrong with your TV?

B: It's just old and suffers from wear and tear.

A: 你的電視怎麼了？

B: 就是老舊和遭受到磨損。

wind down 結束／關掉

A: I think it's about time to wind down watching TV.

B: I think so, too. I have to get up early to attend class tomorrow.

A: 我想該關掉電視的時間到了。

B: 我也這麼想，我明天必須早起去上課。

08 電腦場景

be suitable for 合適的

A：I really like your new iPad. It's very light weight.

B：That's right, and it is suitable for students to use.

A：我很喜歡你的新平板電腦，它的重量很輕。

B：沒錯，它很適合學生使用。

be supplanted by 取代

A：In most offices, the desktop has now been supplanted by the laptop.

B：I think so.

A：在多數辦公室裡，桌上型電腦現在已經逐漸被筆記型電腦取代。

B：我也這樣認為。

be welcome to sth. 可以自由使用

指可以自由隨意使用。

A：Betty is typing her paper on your desktop.

B：She's welcome to it.

A：貝蒂在用你的電腦打她的報告。

B：她可以自由使用。

back up 備份

A：Have you saved your data on a flash drive?

B：I back up my data in the computer every other week.

A：你有把你的資料儲存到隨身碟裡嗎？

B：我每隔一週都會備份我的電腦資料。

補充

every other 每隔。

PART

carry around 隨身攜帶

A：Now the laptop is an essential learning tool for a student.

B：Yes, it is light and easy to carry around.

A：現在筆記型電腦是學生的基本學習工具。

B：沒錯，它很輕且易於隨身攜帶。

cope with 處理

指應付的意思。

A：I don't know how to cope with the computer virus.

B：Fortunately, I know how to handle it.

A：我不知道如何處理電腦病毒。

B：很幸運地，我知道如何處理它。

feed into 輸入

A: The results are fed into a computer. Please check them.

B: I find there are several errors in the input.

A: 結果已輸入電腦裡，請檢查一下。

B: 我發現當中有好幾處錯誤。

hook up 安裝

指安裝收音機、電話機或電腦等等機械設備。

A: I just bought a new computer.

B: Do you need help hooking it up?

A: 我剛買一台新電腦。

B: 你需要幫忙安裝嗎？

PART

infect with 感染

A: Is there anything wrong with the computer?

B: It is infected with a virus.

A: 這電腦有什麼問題？

B: 它感染了病毒。

set up 安裝

A: Why do you look upset?

B: I was setting up the new game in my computer this morning, but the electricity went out.

A: 你為什麼看起來心情不好？

B: 今早我在我的電腦上安裝新遊戲，但後來停電了。

shut down 關機

A: There must be something wrong with the computer. It won't shut down.

B：You might try Andy.

A：電腦一定出毛病了，它不能關機。

B：你可以問一下安迪。

take over 接管

A：Oh, my God. My files in my computer are wiped out. I think a hacker took over my computer.

B：Did you install some firewall software?

A：哦，天啊，我電腦裡的檔案消失了，我認為駭客接管了我的電腦。

B：你有安裝防火牆軟體嗎？

wipe out 清除

A：You only wipe out the virus to save the software in the computer. Got that?

B：I think I got it now.

PART

A：要保護電腦中的軟體，你只能清除病毒，知道了嗎？

B：我想我現在知道了。

09 網路場景

a drag 無趣

drag 是俚語，是「令人厭倦的人或事」，引申爲無趣的意思。

A: Surfing the net is a drag. Let's go shopping tonight.

B: Let's go to the movies instead.

A: 上網很無趣，今晚我們去購物吧。

B: 我們改去看電影吧。

as usual 像往常一樣

指照常、照例或仍然。

A: Do you know where Jane is?

B: Probably surfing the net as usual.

A：你知道珍在哪裡？

B：像往常一樣可能在上網。

at a snail's pace 非常慢

解說

snail's pace 是像蝸牛般的爬行，形容很慢。

A：I have complained that the Internet is moving at a snail's pace.

B：Maybe it is infected with a virus, so you should run a virus scan on your computer first.

A：我要抱怨網路速度太慢了。

B：也許是電腦中毒，所以你應該先對你的電腦進行病毒掃描。

be clogged with 被…塞滿

clog 阻塞。

A: My e-mail is clogged with spam.

B: So is mine. I've just about had enough.

A: 我的電子信箱塞滿了垃圾郵件。

B: 我的也是，我簡直受夠了。

be lost in 沉迷於

A: Andy is lost in surfing the net. His grades have fallen.

B: Someone needs to talk some sense into him.

A: 安迪沉迷於上網，他的成績已經退步了。

B: 有人需要對他講些道理。

be lost in = be addicted to；talk sense 講道理。

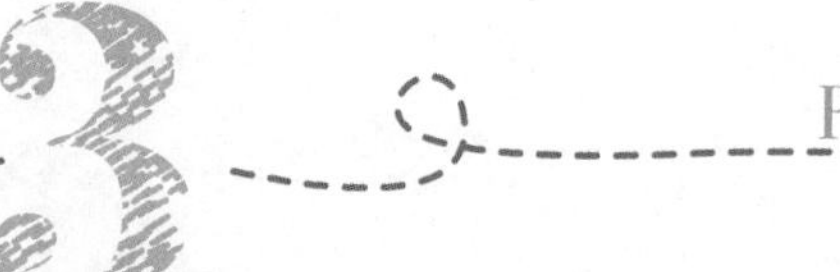

up to date 最新的

A: Surfing the net brings me up to date with current news.

B: No doubt about it. You know everything about everything.

A: 上網帶給我最新的時事。

B: 毫無疑問，你無所不知。

for the first time 第一次

A: I heard you'll meet your Internet friend for the first time.

B: Yes, I have a date tomorrow.

A: 我聽說你第一次跟你的網友見面。

B: 沒錯，我明天有個約會。

get offline 離線

A：I am getting offline. Talk to you later.

B：I will send messages to you, then. Please check it. Thanks.

A：我要離線，以後再談。

B：那麼我送訊息給你，請你看一下，謝謝。

補充

get online 上線。

have a hard time 在…有困難

A：I'm having a hard time playing online games.

B：Let me teach you how to play them.

A：我玩線上遊戲時遇到困難。

B：讓我教你如何玩它們。

in sb.'s hands 在某人控制之下

A: As I surf the net, I feel the world is in my hands.

B: Yeah. You can find out anything you want to know from the Internet.

A: 當我上網時，我覺得世界是在我控制之下。

B: 是啊，你可以從網路找到你想知道的事情。

off the network 網路不通

A: My computer is infected and off the network.

B: Now you finally realized that adding a set of antivirus software to your computer is a must.

A: 我的電腦中毒而且網路不通。

B: 現在你終於意識到安裝一套防毒軟體到你的電腦是必要的。

surf the net 上網

A: After one week of computer lessons, I learned how to surf the net.

B: Like my dad always says: "practice makes perfect".

A: 上了一週電腦課後，我已學會如何上網。

B: 像我爸爸常說：熟能生巧。

補充

surf the net = surf the web = surf the Internet

tear oneself away from 捨不得離開

解說

指離開喜歡的人或物。

A: The computer game is very fun and challenging. Have you played it?

B: I could hardly tear myself away from it lately.

PART

A：這個電腦遊戲非常有趣且富有挑戰性，你玩過嗎？

B：我最近幾乎捨不得離開它。

10 印表機與影印機場景

be used up 用完

A：Peter, the printer can't print the documents.

B：I think the ink is used up.

A：彼得，印表機無法列印文件了。
B：我想墨水用完了。

copying machine 影印機

A：What's the matter with the copying machine?

B：The paper keeps jamming.

A：影印機發生了什麼事？
B：夾紙了。

copying machine = photocopier

PART

go wrong 弄錯

A: The printer does not work properly after changing the cartridge.

B: You need to read the instructions to see where you went wrong.

A: 印表機在換墨水匣後，已經不能正常使用。

B: 你需要閱讀說明書來看你哪裡有問題。

on top 在上面

A: I don't know how to use the photocopier.

B: Why don't you read the instructions on top?

A: 我不知道如何使用影印機。

B: 你為什麼不看上面的指示呢？

paper jam 卡紙

A: The printer is so easy to get a paper jam.

B: It is a good time to buy a new one.

A: 印表機很容易卡紙。
B: 該是買新印表機的時候了。

print out 印出

A: Could I use your printer to print out my report?

B: Sure. But it often doesn't work that well.

A: 我能借你的印表機來列印我的報告嗎？
B: 可以，但是它常故障。

printer settings 列印格式

A: The data range is incorrect. I wish I could correct the problem.

B: Did you check the printer settings to see if it's correct?

A: 資料範圍不正確，我希望我能修正這個問題。
B: 你有檢查印表機設定，看看是否正確嗎？

run off 複印

指印出。

A：I need to run off 100 copies of this article.

B：I will go to the print shop with you.

A：我需要複印這篇文章100份。

B：我會跟你去影印店。

take out 取出

A：How do you clear a paper jam in the printer?

B：It's not a big deal. I'll take them out.

A：如何清除印表機卡紙的問題？

B：這不是一個大問題，我幫你取出來。

warm up 暖機

A: Do you know where that noise is coming from?

B: The printer makes this noise when it's warming up.

A: 你知道那個噪音來自哪裡嗎？

B: 當印表機在暖機時，就會發出這種噪音。

PART

11 電器故障場景

be down 故障

A：How is your term paper coming along?

B：My computer is down, so I haven't been able to work on it.

A：你的學期報告進展的如何？

B：我的電腦故障了，所以不能繼續工作。

beyond repair 無法修理

A：The recorder is out of order. Could you repair it?

B：The parts for this are obsolete, so it's beyond repair.

A：錄音機故障了，你能修理好嗎？

B：錄音機的零件過時了，所以無法修理了。

done for 完蛋了

強調東西毀了。

A: The computer keeps crashing and I have to boot it over and over again.

B: I think it is done for.

A: 電腦一直當機，而我必須不斷地重複開機。

B: 我想電腦完蛋了。

done for 有「累壞了」的意思，I was done for after the match. 在比賽後我累壞了。

get sth. repaired 將某物送修

A: There is something wrong with my computer. It often shuts down by itself.

B: You'd better get it repaired.

A：我的電腦出問題了，它常自動關機。

B：你最好將它送修。

go haywire 故障

指機器失靈；haywire 出毛病。

A：The picture just went blank while I was surfing channels. I think the television went haywire.

B：Maybe it is time to buy a new one.

A：當我轉台時卻沒有畫面，我想電視機故障了。

B：或許到了該買一台新電視機的時候了。

out of order 故障

A：I tried to use the ATM, but it was out of order.

B：I guess you'll have to go to another bank.

A：我試過用ATM，但是它故障了。
B：我想你必須去別家銀行。

put sb.'s finger on 確切地指出

A：I wonder what's wrong with the computer.

B：I think it's something simple, but I just can't put my finger on it.

A：我想知道電腦出了什麼問題。
B：我想問題有點簡單，但是我不能確切地指出。

make a mistake 出差錯

指犯了錯誤。

A：How did so many errors in the poster get by you?

B：I think the computer made a mistake.

A：你怎麼沒有檢查出海報上有這麼多錯呢？

B：我想是電腦出錯了。

get by 通過。

▶▶ on the blink 故障

用在機器、儀表板的故障。

A：I need to type a resume now. Could I use your laptop?

B：I'd love to, but sadly, it's on the blink.

A：我現在需要打一份履歷，我可以使用你的筆記型電腦嗎？

B：我很願意，但是很慘的是它故障了。

on the fritz 發生故障

用在指機器發生故障。

A: The server's down. I set up the operation system again.

B: If you don't install the antivirus software this time, your computer will again be on the fritz.

A: 伺服器壞了，我再次安裝作業系統。

B: 如果你這次沒有安裝防毒軟體，你的電腦會再次發生故障。

under warranty 保固期間

A: My watch is broken.

B: Well, is it still under warranty?

A: 我的手錶壞了。

B: 嗯，它還在保固期間嗎？

PART

▸▸ upside down 顛倒

指上下顛倒。

A: I think the calculator is broken. Finally, I found out I've got the battery upside down.

B: That has happened to me before.

A: 我以為我的計算機壞了，最後才發現電池裝顛倒了。

B: 這種事情以前在我身上發生過。

常形容故障的同義片語有

(1)be broke，The computer is broke. 我的電腦故障了。
(2)be down，The computer is down. 我的電腦故障了。
(3)doesn't work，The computer doesn't work. 我的電腦故障了。
(4)out of order，The computer is out of work. 我的電腦故障了。
(5)have a glitch，The computer has a glitch. 我的電腦故障了。

a blackout 停電

指部分的停電。

A：The storm caused a blackout in the town.

B：Yeah, it was darker than I've seen it before.

A：暴風雨造成了城市停電。

B：沒錯，比我以前見過的更暗。

be home to 所在地

A：What do you think the rainforest is?

B：The rainforest is home to many plants and animals.

A：你認為雨林是什麼呢？

B：雨林是許多動植物的所在地。

PART

▶▶ be on 正開著

A: The furnace is on, but it's still cold in here.

B: It takes some time for the heat to spread throughout the building.

A: 這暖氣是開著的，但是這裡還是很冷。
B: 熱氣要擴散到整個建築物需要一些時間。

▶▶ be sick of 厭倦

A: I'm sick of watching soap operas on TV every night.

B: Maybe you should get a hobby.

A: 我厭倦每晚看肥皂劇。
B: 或許你應該培養一個嗜好。

be sick of = be tired of

▶▶ burn out 燒壞

A: The light bulb in the flashlight has burned out and needs to be replaced.

B: You're wrong. It's because the battery is dead.

A: 手電筒裡的電燈泡燒壞了，需要更換。
B: 你弄錯了，那是因為電池沒電。

▶▶ lose sb.'s way 迷路

A: Where are you?

B: I lost my way to your house. Could you tell me the directions again?

A: 你在哪裡？
B: 我在去你家的路上迷路了，你能告訴我方向嗎？

▶▶ on purpose 故意

A: How stupid of me to break your precious vase.

B: It doesn't matter. I know that you didn't break my vase on purpose.

A: 我很遲鈍，打破你的寶貴花瓶。

B: 沒關係，我知道你不是故意打破我的花瓶。

put up 建造

A: The school is going to tear down the old building and put up a new dormitory.

B: I hope it will be completed before I graduate from school.

A: 這學校會拆毀老的建築物來建造新的宿舍。

B: 我希望新宿舍能在我畢業前建造完成。

power failure 停電

指電源故障或中斷所引起的停電。

A: I experienced a power failure while I was cooking last night.

B: Me, too. I was typing on my computer when it happened.

A: 當我昨晚在煮飯時，碰到了停電。
B: 我也是。停電發生時，我正在用電腦打字。

switch on 開

A: I cannot see anything. Would you mind switching on the light?

B: Not at all.

A: 我看不見任何東西，你介意開燈嗎？
B: 不介意。

turn off 關閉

A: The faucet is leaking. For the life of me, I can't turn it off.

B：Let's call a plumber.

A：水龍頭在漏水，我怎麼也無法關緊它。
B：我們去請水電工來吧。

turn on 打開

A：Whew! It's a scorcher today.

B：I will stay home and turn on the air-conditioner.

A：哇！今天真是個大熱天。
B：我會留在家裡並打開冷氣。

turn up 調高

A：Could you please turn up the heat? It's too cold here.

B：Sure, but you are going to pay for the heating bill.

A：你能不能調高溫度？這裡太冷了。
B：當然可以，不過你要付暖氣費。

PART 

第4單元

行生活片語

01 汽車場景

▶▶ act up 運作不正常

A: My car keeps acting up.

B: It's only a matter of time before it doesn't work again.

A: 我的車子運作不正常。

B: 它再次故障，只是時間問題。

▶▶ be dead 沒電

be dead 前面的主詞是 battery，這裡的 dead 不是死去的意思，而是引申爲沒電。

A: The battery is dead. My car won't start.

B: Wait a moment. I can charge up your car battery.

A: 電池沒電，我的汽車發動不了。

B: 等一下，我可以替你把汽車電瓶充電。

back up 倒退

A: I wish that car would back up a bit so we could pass.

B: Don't worry. I'm sure they will.

A: 我希望那輛車能倒退一點，那樣我們就能通過。
B: 不要擔心，我肯定他們會倒退的。

補充

back up 有「支援」的意思，I back you up. 我支援你。

car sick 暈車

A: Do you get car sick?

B: I will take some medicine just to be on the safe side.

A: 你會暈車嗎？
B: 為了安全起見，我會先吃藥。

補充

air sick 暈機；sea sick 暈船。

fill up 裝滿

A：I need to fill up the gas. How far is the nearest service station?

B：The map shows it's about 3 miles.

A：我需要加滿汽油，最近的加油站是多遠呢？

B：地圖指出約3英里左右。

floor it 加速

A：You'd better floor it if you want to make it to school on time.

B：I'd rather be late than get another speeding ticket.

A：如果你要準時到達學校，你最好加速。

B：我寧願遲到，也不願被開另一張的超速罰單。

flat tire 爆胎

直譯爲「平的輪胎」。

A：What's wrong with your car?

B：I have a flat tire.

A：你的車有什麼問題？
B：我的車爆胎了。

go for a bike ride 騎車兜風

A：I want to go for a bike ride after class. Are you interested?

B：Sorry, I have to meet my brother at the airport.

A：下課後，我要去騎車兜風，你有興趣嗎？
B：抱歉，我必須去機場接我的哥哥。

off the beaten track 偏僻

A: Sorry, it took me so long to get here.

B: No worries. I know it's a bit off the beaten track around here.

A: 對不起，我花了很久時間到達這裡。

B: 沒關係，我知道這附近有點太偏僻了。

run down 沒電

指機器或設備的效能逐漸損耗與降低，而在這裡指電池效能的降低，引申爲沒電。

A: I can't get the car to work.

B: I think the car battery has run down.

A: 我無法使車子發動。

B: 我想是汽車電池沒電了。

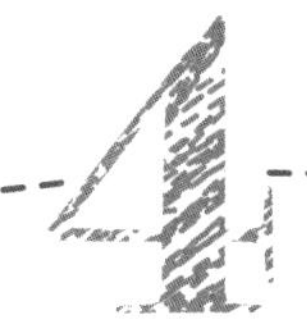

run into 總計

A: The repair fee will run into more than two thousand dollars.

B: It's too expensive. Now you have no other choice except to buy a new one.

A: 這修理費總計超過2,000美元。

B: 太貴了，現在除了買一台新的車子外，你沒有其他選擇。

show off 炫耀

A: Look. Helen is showing off her new car.

B: It is beginning to get annoying.

A: 瞧，海倫正在炫耀她的新車。

B: 開始令人討厭了。

02 塞車場景

at a standstill 停頓

standstill 是停止的意思。

A: Sorry, I was late. There was a car crash on the street and the traffic was at a standstill.

B: It was the same for me. Finally, it took me three hours to get here.

A: 對不起，我遲到了，街道上有一個車禍，交通都停頓了。

B: 我也是一樣，最後我花了三小時才到這裡。

be backed up 阻塞

指交通受到阻礙，而使車輛造成塞車。

A: The traffic is backed up for a few miles. I don't know if I can catch the flight in time.

B：Don't worry. I know a shortcut there.

A：塞車好幾英里，我不知道是否能及時趕上班機。

B：不用擔心，我知道那裡有條捷徑。

be tied up in traffic 塞車

常指意外事件促使交通受到阻礙。

A：Why didn't you get here on time? I thought you forgot our appointment.

B：Sorry, I was tied up in traffic.

A：為什麼你沒有準時到達這裡？我以為你忘了我們的約會。

B：抱歉，我遇到塞車了。

be tied up in traffic = be held up in traffic

bumper to bumper 擁塞

bumper 是保險桿，bumper to bumper 是保險桿碰保險桿，表示車子距離很近，一輛接著一輛，幾乎可以碰到彼此之間的保險桿，也就是塞車才會發生此現象。

A：An accident held up the freeway. The traffic is bumper to bumper for miles.

B：Oh dear.

A：一場意外事件讓高速公路的交通中斷，塞車塞了好幾英里。

B：哦，糟了。

drive sb. out of one's mind 讓某人發瘋

A：The heavy traffic is driving me out of my mind.

B：There is nothing you can do about it.

A：這塞車讓我發瘋。

B：你根本一點辦法也沒有。

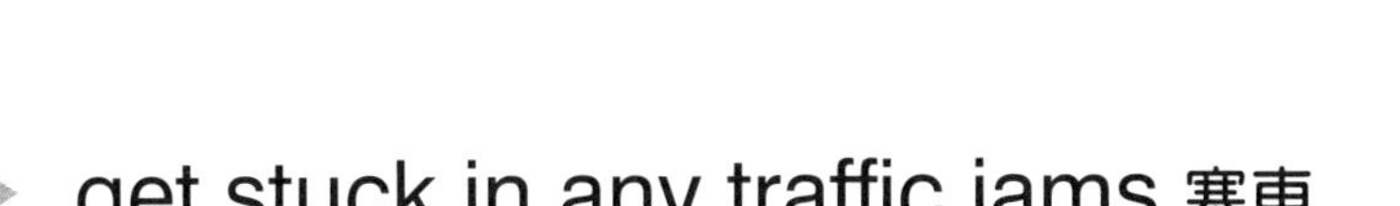

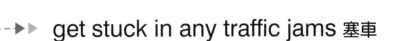

get stuck in any traffic jams 塞車

解說

get stuck in 陷入，traffic jam 是塞車的意思。

A：Leave early tomorrow to avoid getting stuck in any traffic jams.

B：Good idea.

A：明天要提早出門來避開塞車。

B：好主意。

road construction 道路施工

A：I saw signs at the station that there might be some road construction.

B：Yes, I saw those signs, too.

A：我在車站看見有些道路施工標誌。

B：是啊，我也看見那些標誌了。

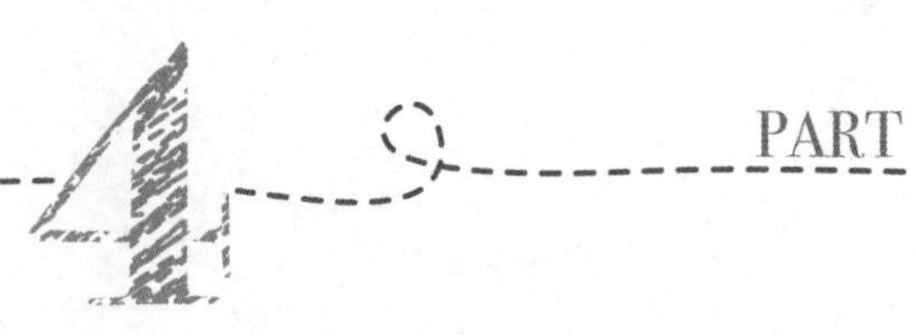

▶▶ road hog 自私的司機

指駕駛人亂開車，且開到其他行車道路上或行駛在道路中央。

A：Look at that idiot driver taking up all the lanes.

B：Road hog.

A：看看那個占據整條馬路的白癡駕駛。

B：自私的司機。

▶▶ rush hour 尖峰時間

指上下班交通最擁擠的時間。

A：I'm always late for my first class. It's because of the heavy traffic during the rush hour.

B：Well, you wouldn't have that problem if you moved onto campus.

A：我經常在第一節課遲到，那是因為在尖峰時間塞車嚴重。

B：嗯，如果你搬到校園來，就不會有那種問題。

▶▶ under construction 正在修建中

A：I heard that they were going to build a new bridge across the river.

B：Yes, it's under construction now.

A：我聽說他們要建造一座橫渡河流的新橋。

B：沒錯，它現在正在修建中。

03 汽車違規場景

▶▶ buckle up 繫上安全帶

尤指汽車內的安全帶。

A: Best buckle up in case a cop sees you.

B: Yeah, I've been pulled over before for not wearing a seat belt.

A: 最好是繫上你的安全帶，以免被警察看到。

B: 對啊，我之前有被警察攔下來，就是因為沒繫安全帶。

▶▶ car crash 車禍

指汽車撞車事故。

A: I saw a nasty car crash on the freeway today.

B: Oh, no! Was anyone hurt?

A：我今天在高速公路上看到一場嚴重的車禍。
B：不會吧！有沒有人受傷呢？

drive over the speed limit 超速行駛

A: I got a ticket for speeding.

B: You shouldn't drive over the speed limit, or you will have to pay fines for speeding.

A：我接到超速罰單。
B：你不應該超速行駛，否則你必須支付超速的罰款。

give sb. a ticket 給某人開罰單

原意為給某人一張票，引申為給某人開罰單。

A: The state patrol gave me a ticket for speeding to teach me a lesson.

B：That was a costly experience.

A：公路巡邏警察給我開了一張超速罰單來教訓我。

B：那真是一個「昂貴」的代價。

▶▶ hit-and-run 肇事逃逸的

A：My friend was killed by a hit-and-run driver crossing the road last week.

B：You must be careful in crossing the street later.

A：我的朋友上星期在過馬路時，被肇事逃逸的司機撞死了。

B：你以後在過街道時，一定要留神。

▶▶ parking ticket 違規停車罰單

A：Today is not my day! I got a parking ticket.

B：I guess you must have parked in a place where you shouldn't have.

A：今天不是我的好日子！我被開了違規停車罰單。

B：我想你一定停在不該停的地方。

pick up speed 加快速度

pick up 增加。

A：Oh, no! The meeting's going to start in less than ten minutes.

B：We'd better pick up some speed or will miss the start of it.

A：糟了！這會議不到10分鐘就要開始了。

B：我們最好加快速度，否則會錯過會議的開幕儀式。

pull over 開到路邊

A：The cop pulled me over and gave me a ticket. Do you know why?

B：Let me guess. You were speeding again.

A：警察叫我開到路邊，給我開了一張罰單，你知道為什麼嗎？

B：我猜，你又超速了。

run through a red light 闖紅燈

run through 穿過。

A：I saw a car running through a red light today right in front of a police car.

B：What an idiot!

A：我今天看到一輛車子在警車面前闖紅燈。

B：真是一個笨蛋！

▶▶ slow down 慢下來

指減速。

A: The speed bumps seem to work very well on the one-way street.

B: Yeah. They slow down the cars very effectively.

A: 在單行道上道路減速板似乎非常有用。

B: 是啊，它們非常有效地讓車子慢下來。

speed bump = sleeping policeman 道路減速板，指的是道路上使車輛減速的減速板。

▶▶ tow away 拖吊離開

A: I'm sorry to hear that your car was towed away in the parking lot.

B: It was my fault as I didn't realize that my student parking sticker had expired.

PART

A：我很遺憾地聽到你的車在停車場被拖走。

B：都是我的錯，因為我沒有意識到我的學生停車證已經過期。

04 搭車場景

▶▶ behind schedule 晚點

解說

behind 在…之後；schedule 時間表。

A：The bus is running behind schedule. I'm afraid I can't make the 7:15 movie.

B：Why don't you take a taxi there?

A：巴士誤點，我擔心無法趕上7點15分的電影。
B：你為什麼不搭計程車去那裡呢？

▶▶ drop off 讓…下車

A：Could you drop off the kids near the school?

B：Sure, no problem.

A：你可以讓小孩在學校附近下車嗎？
B：當然，沒問題。

exact change 不找零錢

A: The bus will only accept exact change.

B: Do you have change for a ten-dollar bill?

A: 這種公車是不找零的。

B: 你有十元的零錢可換嗎？

exact change = keep change

get on 上車

A: I'll get on the bus at nine o'clock tomorrow.

B: Then you had better have your small change ready.

A: 我明天早上九點要搭公車。

B: 那麼最好準備好你的零錢。

get off 下車

A：Where do I get off the bus?

B：You get off the bus at the next stop.

A：我要在何處下車呢？
B：你要在下一個公車站下車。

get out 下車

指從某處出來。

A：Let's get out of the car.

B：Remember that we must take the baggage to our room.

A：我們下車吧。
B：記住，我們必須拿行李到我們的房間。

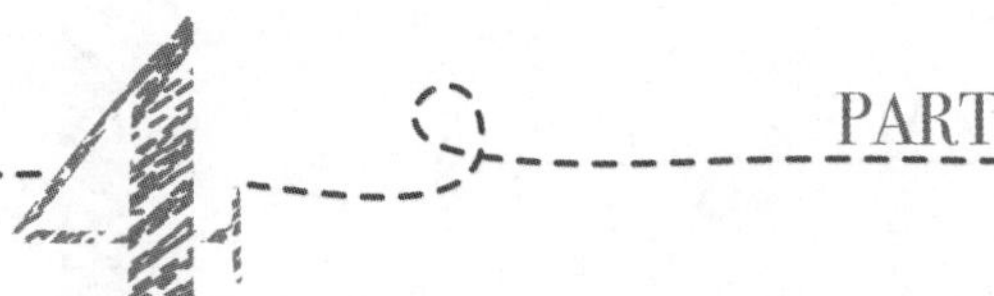

give sb. a lift 搭便車

A：Can you give me a lift to the post office?

B：Hop in. We are both going the same way.

A：你可以讓我搭便車到郵局嗎？

B：上車吧，我們是同路的。

give sb. a ride 搭便車

ride 是乘坐的意思。

A：Sorry, I have to go, or I'm going to miss the school bus.

B：Don't worry about that. If you can't catch that one, I could give you a ride.

A：抱歉，我必須走了，否則我會搭不上校車。

B：別擔心那個，如果你趕不上，我可以讓你搭便車。

give sb. a ride = give sb. a lift

hitch a ride 搭便車

指搭車是完全免費。

A：My car's being repaired. Now I badly need to hitch a ride to school.

B：You can try Peter. I know there is room in Peter's car.

A：我的車正在修理，現在我非常需要搭便車到學校。

B：你可以問彼得，我知道彼得車裡有空位。

hop in 快點上車

A：Could you give us a lift to the Metropolitan Museum?

B：Yes, of course. Hop in.

A：你能讓我們搭便車到大都會博物館嗎？

B：是的，可以，快點上車。

補充

小汽車上車用 hop in、get in 或 jump in，下車用 get out；大巴士上車用 get on，下車用 get off。

lost and found 失物招領處

A：I lost my camera on the bus last night.

B：That happened to me once. I found it at the lost and found.

A：我昨晚在公車上遺失了照相機。

B：這種事情曾經發生在我身上，我在失物招領處找到了它。

▶▶ pull away 離開

指交通工具的離開。

A: Hurry up; the train will pull away from the station in a minute.

B: I'm coming as fast as I can.

A: 快一點，這班火車馬上要開了。
B: 我正努力趕來。

▶▶ stop off 短暫停留

A: I think we need to stop off in Taichung first.

B: Do you want to visit the gallery?

A: 我想我們必須先在臺中做短暫停留。
B: 你想要參觀美術館嗎？

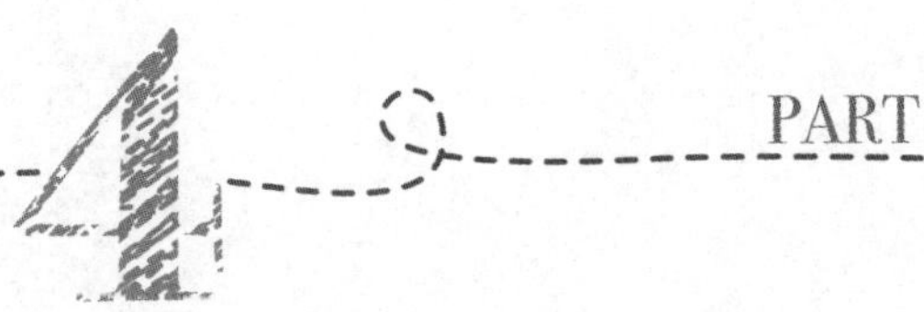

▸▸ thumb a ride 搭便車

豎起拇指爲手勢，向路過的車輛要求搭便車。

A: Ann always thumbs a ride to school to save money on the public transportation fare.

B: She is on a tight budget since she got a loan to buy a new house.

A: 安為了省公共交通費，經常搭便車到學校。

B: 自從她貸款買了一棟新房子後，她手頭就很緊。

05 飛機場景

be booked up 客滿

A：The flights to Vancouver are all booked up.

B：You'd better call your brother, and tell him you can't make it there tonight.

A：到溫哥華班機已經全客滿了。

B：你最好打電話給你哥哥，告訴他你今晚不能到達那裡。

carry-on baggage 隨身行李

A：How much carry-on baggage am I allowed?

B：You can bring one piece only, with a maximum weight of 8kg.

A：我可以帶多少隨身行李呢？

B：你只可以帶一件隨身行李，最大重量8公斤。

▸▸ checked baggage 託運行李

A: Your checked baggage is over the allowance.

B: What are the charges for being overweight?

A: 你的託運行李超過限額了。
B: 超重費是多少？

▸▸ for hours on end 連續好幾小時

A: I have been waiting for the plane to arrive for hours on end.

B: I hate delayed flights.

A: 我連續好幾小時等待飛機抵達。
B: 我討厭誤點的班機。

▸▸ kill time 消磨時間

A: The airline announced that the flight is delayed for three hours.

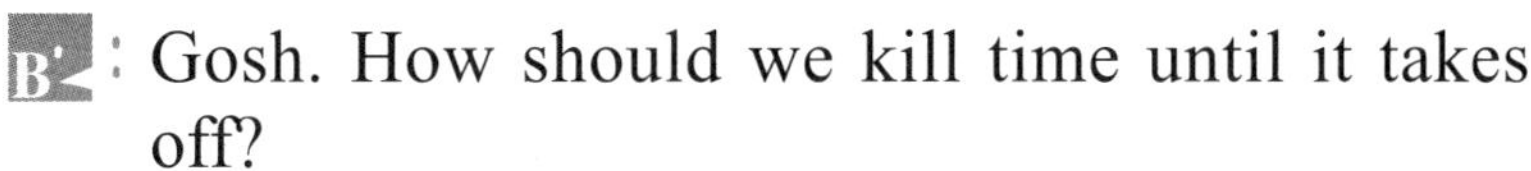

B：Gosh. How should we kill time until it takes off?

A：航空公司宣布這班機誤點3小時。

B：天啊，飛機起飛前，我們該如何消磨時間呢？

補充

kill time = count sb.'s thumbs

on sb.'s way 在路途中

A：What time will you arrive here?

B：I'm on my way over now.

A：什麼時候你會到達這裡？

B：我現在正在前往的路途中。

pick sb. up 接某人

A：Could you pick me up at the airport tomorrow night?

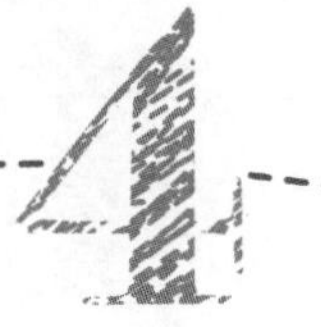

B: I won't be off work until 9:00 pm tomorrow. Will that be too late?

A: 你明天晚上能到機場接我嗎？

B: 我明天晚上9點才會下班，那會不會太晚呢？

put off 延後

A: Thc trip has to be put off because the blizzard blocked all the roads to the airport.

B: It's a shame that we have to cancel this trip.

A: 旅行不得不延後，因為暴風雪阻斷所有去機場的道路。

B: 我們必須取消這次旅行，真遺憾。

put off = hold off = delay = postpone = suspend

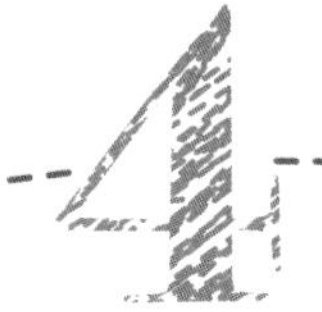

sell out 賣完

A: The airline informed us that the flight is sold out.

B: It seems like I need to look for some activities to tide me over this weekend.

A: 航空公司通知我們，機票已賣完了。

B: 看來我需要尋找一些活動來度過這個週末。

tide sb. over (sth.) 度過；克服。

step on it 快一點

A: Could you step on it, please? I have a plane to catch at three.

B: Well, now it's rush hour and I cannot control the flow of traffic.

A: 請你能不能快一點？我要趕三點的飛機。

B: 喔，現在是交通尖峰時間，我不能控制車流量。

stop over 中途逗留

A：I will stop over at Kyoto for sightseeing on my way home.

B：It seems like a good idea.

A：在回國途中，我將在京都中途逗留，進行觀光遊覽。

B：那似乎是個好主意。

take off 起飛

A：When will the airplane take off ?

B：It's up to the weather.

A：飛機何時要起飛呢？

B：視天氣而定。

06 其他行場景

be off to 到…地方去

A：Where are you off to now?

B：I'm going to visit friends.

A：你現在要去哪裡？

B：我要去拜訪朋友。

catch up with 趕上

A：Why don't you go ahead and I'll catch up with you later?

B：Ok, we will meet you at the mall at 8:00 pm.

A：你為什麼不先走，我隨後就會趕上你？

B：好的，八點我們將在購物中心跟你碰面。

PART

come along 跟隨

跟另外一個人走。

A: I'm going to the basketball court. Do you want to come along with me?

B: No, I'm talking about my assignment with classmates on LINE.

A: 我正要去籃球場，你想要跟我去嗎？

B: 不，我正在用LINE跟同學談論作業。

come back 回來

A: I am going to New York next week.

B: When will you come back?

A: 下週我要去紐約。

B: 你何時回來呢？

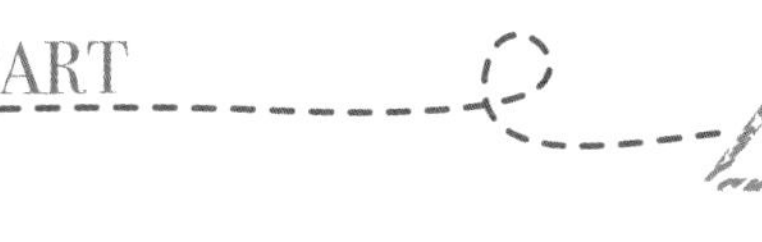

come back = get back

come over 過來

指順便來訪。

A: Would you like to come over and watch a movie?

B: I'll be over after I eat dinner.

A: 你想要過來看電影嗎？

B: 我吃完晚餐後，就會過去。

get moving 趕快

A: We've got just an hour before the train arrives in the station.

B: Let's get moving, or we'll miss the train.

A：在火車到達車站前，我們只有一小時時間。

B：我們快一點吧，否則會趕不上火車。

go by 經過

指從某地點經過。

A：Could you tell me which bus goes by the mall?

B：Sorry, I'm a stranger myself here.

A：你能告訴我哪一輛公車會經過購物中心嗎？

B：抱歉，我自己對這裡也不熟。

go up to 前往

A：Have you any plans over the spring break?

B：Well, I'm really expecting to go up to California for a few days.

A：你在春假有任何計畫嗎？
B：嗯，我很期待前往加州幾天。

make a run into town 到城裡去

run 短期旅行或訪問。

A：I have to make a run into town today for groceries and other supplies.

B：What a coincidence, so do I.

A：我今天必須到城裡去買食品與其他日常用品。
B：真巧，我也是。

on the corner 在轉角處

指在角落上的外角。

A: I've been standing on the corner for over an hour waiting for a bus.

B: The bus doesn't run this route on weekends.

A: 我一直站在轉角處等待公車超過了一小時。
B: 每逢週末公車沒有跑這條路線。

rely on 依賴

A: You can't rely on the schedule of buses during rush hour.

B: The traffic is heavy at that time of day, I know.

A: 在尖峰時間，你不能依賴公車的時刻表。
B: 我知道，在一天中的那段時間塞車很嚴重。

walk up 走上

指向上走。

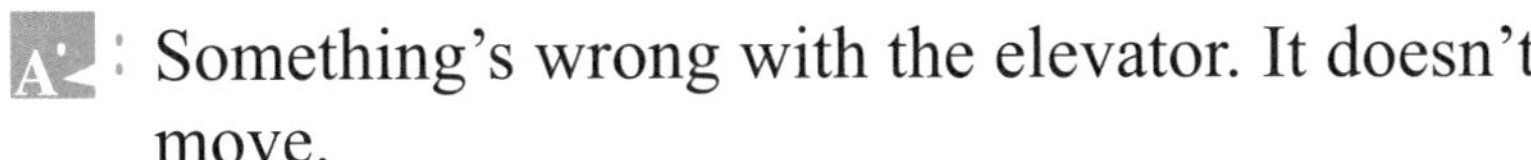

A: Something's wrong with the elevator. It doesn't move.

B: I guess we can walk up the stairs.

A: 這電梯故障了，它不能動了。

B: 我想我們可以順著樓梯走上去。

PART

育生活片語

01 學習過程場景

02 學習忙碌場景

03 學習忘記場景

04 圖書館場景

05 書店場景

06 學習累場景

07 學習瞭解場景

08 學習簡單與困難場景

09 學習擅長與專心場景

01 學習過程場景

▶▶ a case in point 適當的例子

指合適與明顯的例子。

A: Frankly, the concept sounds lame.

B: Let me see. I will demonstrate a case in point later.

A: 坦白地說，這個觀念聽起來沒有說服力。

B: 讓我想一想，稍後我會示範一個適當的例子。

▶▶ be finished 做完

A: I'm finished with the term paper.

B: Under no circumstances will I ever take that teacher again.

A: 我做完了學期報告。

B: 無論如何，我不會再上那位老師的課。

be finished = be done = be over

be through 做完

A：I will be through with my term project tonight.

B：By then. I'll be done, too.

A：我今晚會做完我的學期報告。
B：到那時，我也會做完了。

beef up 加強

A：I am entering a weightlifting competition.

B：You'd better start going to the gym, so you can beef up in time.

A：我要參加一個舉重比賽。
B：你最好開始去健身房，那麼你才來得及加強。

PART

brush up on sth. 複習

A: Do you want to go to the beach?

B: I'd love to, but I need to brush up on my French before taking the test tomorrow.

A: 你想要去海灘嗎？

B: 我很想去，不過在明天考試前，我必須複習我的法語。

build up 加強

A: Why do you often go to the Japanese club after class?

B: I want to build up my Japanese communication skills.

A: 你為什麼下課後常去日語社呢？

B: 我想要加強日語溝通技巧。

call on 要求

用在要學生回答問題時。

A: The teacher always calls on Betty to answer questions in class.

B: Everyone knows she is the teacher's favorite pupil.

A: 上課中老師經常要貝蒂回答問題。
B: 每個人都知道她是老師最喜歡的學生。

catch up on sth. 趕完

指做尚未完成的事，強調彌補某件事情。

A: Are you caught up on your assignment before you go to bed?

B: Not yet, but now I would like to get some air outside.

A：你在睡覺前，會趕完你的作業嗎？

B：還沒有，但是現在我想要到外面透透氣。

▶▶ come up with sth. 提出

指提出建議、想法或計畫。

A：I need to come up with a better plan next time.

B：I agree. You should have more evidence to support your plan.

A：下次我需要提出更好的計畫。

B：我同意，你應該要有更多的證據來支持你的計畫。

▶▶ go over 複習

A：Would you like to come to the movies with us?

B：Sounds like a plan. But I've got to go over my notes for tomorrow's finals.

A：你想要跟我們去看電影嗎？

B：聽起來很不錯，但是我必須為明天期末考複習我的筆記。

plough through 費勁地閱讀

plough 爲苦讀的意思，爲美式用法；而英式用法爲 plow。

A：I've been trying plough through this book in a short amount of time.

B：I've been trying, too. But, who can read it and be finished in a week?

A：我一直努力在很短的時間內費勁地閱讀這本書。

B：我也一直在努力，但是，誰能在一星期內讀完它？

pore over 仔細閱讀

pore 熟讀或深思。

A: Are you always staying at the library after class?

B: Yes, I have to pore over my books and work on my papers.

A: 下課後，你總是留在圖書館嗎？

B: 是的，我必須仔細閱讀我的書和寫我的報告。

pick up 學會

用在沒有正式上課而學習到。

A: I want to pick up Japanese on my own.

B: Learning Japanese is not easy. I prefer learning it in school.

A：我要自己學日文。
B：學日文很不容易，我寧願在學校學日文。

spell out 清楚說明

A：Your article I'm interested in is very instructive.

B：I could spell out my views for you now.

A：我對你的文章感興趣，它很有教育性。
B：我現在可以為你清楚說明我的觀點。

speak out 大聲說。

start out 出發（開始著手）

A：Learning English is very easy.

B：I think you start out with the basics, so you think it is very easy.

A：學英文是很簡單的。
B：我想你是從基礎開始，所以你才認為它很簡單。

▶▶ study group 讀書會

A：Could you hold the study group in your apartment?

B：Sure, but I've got to ask my roommate for permission in advance before I say yes.

A：你能在你的公寓舉行讀書會嗎？
B：可以，但是在我說「答應」前，我必須先得到我室友的同意。

▶▶ teacher's pet 老師最喜歡的學生

字面上翻譯爲「老師的寵物」，引申爲老師最喜歡的學生。

A：I think he is a teacher's pet.

B：That's because he is doing well at school.

A：我想他是老師最喜歡的學生。
B：那是因為他在學校功課很好。

tell apart 分辨

A：Frogs and toads all look alike. Sometime I can't tell them apart.

B：Frogs have slippery skin while toads have dry-rough skin.

A：青蛙很像蟾蜍。有時候我無法分辨牠們。
B：青蛙有光滑的皮膚，然而蟾蜍有粗乾的皮膚。

think straight 清晰思考

A：I can't think straight with the noise.

B：Sorry, I will keep it down.

A：因為這噪音，我不能清晰思考。
B：對不起，我會降低音量。

touch on 談到

指關係到。

A：The article doesn't touch on the heart of the topic.

B：Just as I suspected. Your view is the same as mine.

A：這篇文章沒有談到主題的核心。

B：果然不出我所料，你的觀點跟我一樣。

train of thought 思路

A：Do you understand my train of thought?

B：Well, could you make it clear for me again?

A：你能明白我的思路嗎？

B：嗯，你能為我再次解釋它嗎？

make clear 解釋。

transfer to 轉學

A：I'm planning to transfer to Harvard University to complete my degree.

B：That's great. But you must have excellent grades to get into that school.

A：我正計畫轉學到哈佛大學來完成我的學業。

B：那太好了，但是你必須以優秀成績來進入那所學校。

swift major 轉系。

with flying colors 出色地

指獲得成功或得到勝利。

A：You will pass with flying colors.

B：I think so, too. My labor will not be lost.

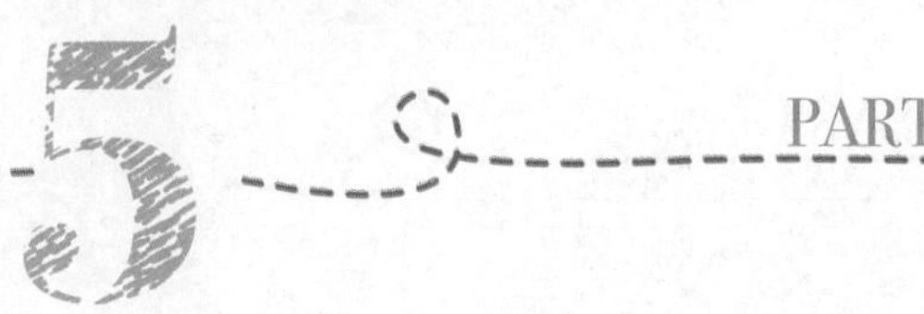

A：你會高分通過考試。

B：我也這樣認為，我的努力不會白費。

02 學習忙碌場景

as busy as a bee 像蜜蜂一樣忙碌

A：I have a hundred things to do. Is there something you can help me with?

B：Sorry, I'm as busy as a bee right now.

A：我有許多事情要做，你能幫我做一些嗎？

B：對不起，我現在很忙。

be busy with 忙於

A：I'll be busy with my finals until next week.

B：So will I. Good luck to us both.

A：在下週之前，我都在忙我的期末考試。

B：我也是，祝我們兩人都好運。

PART

▶▶ be in the middle of sth. 忙於

A：Professor, have you finished reading my proposal?

B：I am in the middle of something right now. Can you come by my office later?

A：教授，你有讀完我的計畫書嗎？

B：我現在正在忙一些事情，你能稍後再來我的辦公室嗎？

▶▶ be occupied with 忙著做

A：Could you teach me arithmetic?

B：I'm occupied with my papers all morning. What do you say to this afternoon?

A：你能教我數學嗎？

B：整個上午我忙著做我的報告，你覺得今天下午怎麼樣呢？

be overwhelmed with 忙著做

A: I heard Susan has been putting in an awful lot of time at the library recently.

B: Well. She is overwhelmed with all the papers.

A：我聽到蘇珊最近花了很多時間在圖書館裡。
B：嗯，她忙著做所有的報告。

be swamped with 忙於

A: I'm always swamped with tests and papers, and I don't have a minute to myself.

B: I hate to say this, but I told you so.

A：我總是忙著考試與報告，我連一點自己的時間也沒有。
B：我很討厭這樣說，但是我早就告訴過你會如此。

be tied up 很忙

指忙得不可開交。

A: I wonder if you will be free to join us.

B: Sorry, I'm all tied up right now.

A: 我想知道是否你有空加入我們。

B: 對不起，我現在很忙。

be up to sb.'s ears 很忙

ears 可用 neck、eyes 或 head 代替，意思一樣。

A: Would you like to play hockey after school?

B: I'd love to, but I'm up to my ears in homework.

A: 放學後，你想玩曲棍球嗎？

B: 我很想玩，但是我正忙著做我的回家作業。

have sb.'s hands full 忙得不可開交

A：Helen, would you like to attend the cocktail party with me today?

B：I'm afraid not. I have my hands full at the moment. I must turn in my biology paper tomorrow.

A：海倫，今天你想要跟我去參加雞尾酒會嗎？

B：我恐怕不行，我目前忙得不可開交，我明天必須交生物報告。

have many irons in the fire 同時有許多事情要做

A：Don't bother me because I'm currently sorting and dating all of documents.

B：You have many irons in the fire so to speak today.

A：不要打擾我，因為我目前正在分類檔案和註明檔案日期。

B：可以說你今天同時有許多事情要做。

in a hurry 很忙

是指很匆忙。

A：Do you have a minute to talk?

B：Actually, I am in a hurry. Can you wait until later?

A：你有空和我談談嗎？

B：事實上，我很忙，能等一會兒嗎？

on the go 忙著不停

go 進行。

A：My dad is a busy man, and is always on the go.

B：At least you can spend time with him on the weekends.

A：我爸爸是很忙碌的人，經常忙個不停。

B：至少每個週末你可以跟他在一起。

03 學習忘記場景

absent-minded 心不在焉

A: Mike is an absent-minded person. He never follows directions.

B: He is a scatterbrain, and is always forgetting something.

A: 麥克是一個心不在焉的人，他從不聽從指示。

B: 他是個糊塗蟲，總是忘記一些東西。

be terrible with 不擅長記憶

A: I hope you'll remember the process of vertebrate evolution.

B: But I'm terrible with vertebrates.

A: 我希望你能牢記脊椎動物的演化過程。

B: 但是我不擅長記憶脊椎動物。

▸▸ be not good with sth. 不擅長記憶

A：My name is Peter. Haven't I met you somewhere before?

B：Sorry, I don't think I've ever met you before and I'm not good with names.

A：我叫彼得，我是不是以前在什麼地方見過你呢？

B：抱歉，我想我從來沒見過你，而且我不擅長記憶名字。

▸▸ go out of sb.'s mind 忘記

A：The doctor asked you to take the pills after meals, but his words often go out of my mind.

B：I'm also a scatterbrain, you know.

A：醫生要你飯後吃藥，但是我常忘記他的話。

B：你知道，我也是一位糊裡糊塗的人。

have a memory like a sieve

記憶力極差

記憶力就像過濾器那麼小，以 sieve 來代表記憶力極差，而類似說法有 have a head like a sieve；而記憶力很好則用大象做代表，如 have a memory like an elephant，表示記憶力特別好。

A：Look at the picture. Do you know the beautiful girl who is wearing a red shirt in the picture?

B：I don't remember who she was. I have a memory like a sieve lately.

A：請看這張相片，你知道在相片裡穿紅色襯衫的美麗女孩是誰嗎？

B：我記不起來她是誰，我最近記憶力極差。

lose count 不清楚

lose 錯過，count 數。

A: Since your boyfriend transferred to another school, how many love letters have you received?

B: I have lost count, but so far, the number is definitely over thirty.

A: 自從你的男友轉學到其他學校，你收到多少情書呢？

B: 我記不清楚了。但是目前為止，這數目明確超過30封。

▶▶ lose track of time 忘記時間

A: I'm really sorry to lose track of time.

B: I've been waiting for you for over an hour.

A: 我很抱歉忘記時間了。

B: 我一直等你超過了一個小時以上。

My mind is not registering.
我的腦子記不住

mind 頭腦，register 記錄。

A：I'm tired out. My mind is not registering everything.

B：Maybe you should get some rest.

A：我很累，我的頭腦記不住任何東西。

B：或許你應該休息一下了。

on the tip of sb.'s tongue 忘記

在舌頭的尖端，表示話快要說出口了，卻忘記了。

A：Do you know the author of "Hamlet"?

B：It's on the tip of my tongue.

A：你知道哈姆雷特的作者嗎？

B：我忘記了。

in one ear and out the other

心不在焉

指當作耳邊風，左耳進右耳出，引申為心不在焉。

A：What did you think of Tom's speech?

B：I wasn't paying attention. It all went in one ear and out the other.

A：你認為湯姆的演講怎麼樣呢？

B：我沒有注意聽，我心不在焉。

in one ear and out the other = go in one ear and out of the other

04 圖書館場景

apply for 申請

A: I don't have a library card, so I can't borrow the books now.

B: You can apply for a library card online and pick up your card when you visit the library.

A: 我沒有借書證，所以我現在不能借書。
B: 你可以線上申請借書證，然後去圖書館時，再取你的借書證。

be overdue 過期的

A: I'm afraid your book is four days overdue.

B: I know I have to pay the fines.

A: 恐怕你的書過期4天了。
B: 我知道我必須支付罰金。

PART

check in 還書

A: I want to avoid paying overdue charges. Would you like to accompany me to the library to check in these books?

B: I'd be happy to go.

A: 我想要避免付逾期罰款，你要不要一起去圖書館歸還這些書呢？

B: 我很樂意跟隨。

check in = return

check out 借書

A: I need a guidebook for the trip.

B: I recommend checking out the book in the library if you want to save money.

A: 我需要一本旅行指南。

B: 如果你想要省錢，我推薦在圖書館借書。

check out = borrow

circulation desk 借書處

A: May I use the computer to look for some information?

B: Sure. But first you need to sign in at the circulation desk.

A: 我能使用電腦尋找資料嗎？

B: 當然可以，但是首先你必須在借書處登記。

fill out 填寫

A: Excuse me. I would like to have a library card.

B: Please fill out this application form and I will create a card for you.

A: 打擾一下，我想要辦理借書證。

B: 請填寫申請表格，我會為你製作借書證。

free access to 免費使用

A: The Professor said all students may have free access to the library resources.

B: You said it. We are free to use the library.

A: 教授說所有學生都可以免費使用圖書館資源。

B: 沒錯，我們可以隨意使用圖書館。

off the shelf 不在架上

A: The book is off the shelf. Can you check out the computer records to see if it's checked out?

B: The book is checked out, and it should be returned tomorrow.

A: 這本書不在架上，你能檢查一下電腦紀錄並且看是否它已經被借走了？

B: 這本書已被借出，應該明天會歸還。

on the shelf 在架上

A：I can't get at the book on the shelf. Do you have a ladder?

B：Yes, I will get the ladder for you.

A：我拿不到架子上的書，你們有梯子嗎？

B：有，我去拿給你。

look up 查詢

A：I can look up for you the encyclopedia after class.

B：Thanks. That would be great.

A：下課後，我可以為你查詢百科全書。

B：謝謝你，那太好了。

refer to 查閱

A：The library is closed today.

B: That is only a minor setback. We can surf the Internet and refer to the online journal databases.

A: 今天圖書館不開放。

B: 那只是小障礙，我們可以上網查閱線上期刊資料庫。

refer to = look up

subscribe to 訂閱

A: You don't need to subscribe to the business magazine. You can read it in the library for free.

B: But that would be an inconvenience.

A: 你不需要訂閱商業期刊，你可以在圖書館免費閱讀。

B: 但是那會很不方便。

track down 尋找

用在必須借用工具來尋找。

A: I found a useful abstract but I would like to get the full-text.

B: You could check with a librarian at the reference desk to learn how to track it down.

A: 我發現了一篇有用的摘要，但我想要得到全文。

B: 你可以詢問在查詢臺的圖書管理員，學會怎樣尋找。

05 書店場景

best seller 暢銷書

A：Have you heard that J.K. Rowling is the author of the best seller "Harry Potter"?

B：Of course. Her novels have a strong student following.

A：你有聽過暢銷書「哈利波特」的作者J.K.羅琳嗎？

B：當然有，她的小說深受學生歡迎。

in print 已出版

指正在發售，可買得到，沒有絕版。

A：The book is no longer in print.

B：I heard that sales are poor.

A：這本書已不再出版。

B：我聽說銷售量不好。

in stock 存貨

A: The book you want to buy is always out of stock.

B: I don't know when it will be back in stock.

A: 你想要買的這本書總是缺貨。
B: 我不知道何時會有存貨。

out of print 已絕版

指不再印刷，已售完。

A: I need a copy of Harry Potter.

B: The book you speak of is out of print.

A: 我要一本哈利波特。
B: 你說的這本書已絕版。

5 

PART

out of stock 缺貨

A: The book is out of stock now.

B: I found out the store was selling off the stock last week.

A: 這本書現在缺貨。

B: 我知道上週這家商店清倉大拍賣這本書。

second-hand 二手

A: My book is really cheap.

B: I think you must have bought it from a second-hand bookshop.

A: 我的書真的很便宜。

B: 我想你一定是在二手書店買到它的。

sell off 廉價出售

A: The publisher will do whatever it takes to sell off all of the books.

B：So, we'd better act fast, before we miss out.

A：出版社不計代價要廉價出售所有的書。
B：所以，在我們錯失機會之前，最好儘快行動。

sell out 賣光

A：Sorry, the math books were sold out. Maybe you need to wait for a few days.

B：Okay. When the books come in, give me a call and I'll come back again.

A：對不起，數學書賣光了，或許你需要等待幾天。
B：好的，當書來時，打電話給我，我會再回來。

take the problem up with 向某人提出問題要求處理

A：I found the book I ordered is damaged. How do I deal with that?

B：You should take the problem up with the shipper.

A：我發現我訂購的書受到損毀，我該如何處理呢？
B：你應該向送貨員提出要求處理。

補充

deal with = cope with

thrift store 二手店

A：I am taking an American Literature class this semester, and the textbook is 70 bucks.

B：What an expensive price. You'd better check out thrift stores to see if they sell it.

A：我這學期修美國文學課，而教科書是70美元。
B：好貴的價格啊。你最好看一下二手書店是否有在賣。

wait in line 排隊等候

A：The book store is crowded, and there is a long line of people in front of the counter.

B：Let's not waste our time waiting in line to buy the book.

A：這家書店很擁擠，人們在櫃檯前排著長長的隊伍。

B：我們不要浪費時間排隊等候買這本書。

wait in line = wait in a queue

06 學習累場景

be beat 很累

A: I have been working on my theory proposal for so long that I'm completely beat.

B: You take a little time off and come to the movies with us tonight.

A: 我花了很久的時間做我的論文計畫書，以致於我很累。

B: 你休息一下，今晚跟我們去看電影吧。

be beat = be bushed = be exhausted = be pooped

be dog-tired 很累

A: I need to take a break. I'm dog-tired.

B: No wonder you are looking off color today.

A: 我需要休息一下，我很累。

B: 難怪你今天看起來氣色不好。

be exhausted 很累

A: I fainted because I was exhausted.

B: You need to catch up on some sleep badly.

A：我頭暈，因為我很累。
B：你很需要補充一些睡眠。

be out of steam 很累

A: It's into the wee hours. I keep thinking how to finish the computer program.

B: You had better go to bed soon, or you will be out of steam tomorrow.

A：已經凌晨了，我一直在想如何完成電腦程式。
B：你最好快上床睡覺，否則你明天會很累。

be out of steam = be out of energy

be out of energy 很累

A：I'm out of energy. I can hardly stay awake.

B：Me, too. Let's go home.

A：我很累，我幾乎不能保持清醒。

B：我也是，我們回家吧。

be tired out 很累

是形容身體精疲力竭。

A：I was extremely tired out after studying all night.

B：Be careful, staying up too much can be bad for your body.

A：整晚的熬夜之後，我很累。

B：要小心，熬夜太多可能對你的身體不好。

▸▸ be wiped out 累壞了

A：I've been studying for the past 12 hours.

B：You must be wiped out.

A：在過去的12小時裡，我一直在讀書。
B：你一定累壞了。

be wiped out = be rundown = be tired out = be dog-tired

▸▸ knock out 很累

指精疲力竭，很累的意思。

A：I tried to call you last night, but your mom said you were knocked out.

B：Yeah. I had been studying for 10 hours straight.

A：我昨晚打電話給你，但是你媽媽說你很累。
B：沒錯，我連續讀書10小時。

PART

▶▶ run-down 累

指精疲力竭的累。

A：The quality of the paper leaves much to be desired and you need to proofread it again.

B：I feel too run-down to do anything more.

A：這份報告的品質有待改進，而你需要再校對一次。

B：我覺得太累了，以致於不能再做任何事情。

▶▶ wear out 筋疲力盡

指很累的樣子。

A：I'm worn out after working on the paper.

B：Well, at least it's over now.

A：做完報告後，我已經筋疲力盡了。

B：嗯，至少現在一切都結束了。

07 學習瞭解場景

be familiar with 熟悉

解說

be familiar with 某人熟悉某物，必須以人爲主詞；be familiar to 某物對某人來說很熟悉，必須以物爲主詞。

A：Are you familiar with the study of anthropology?

B：Yes, I am. I'm an anthropologist.

A：你對人類學研究熟悉嗎？

B：是的，我很熟悉。我是一位人類學家。

be in the picture 瞭解情況

解說

直譯爲「在相片裡面」，引申爲知道詳情與熟悉一切狀況。

A：Are you in the picture?

B：Everyone is in the picture except for Betty.

A：你瞭解情況嗎？

B：除了貝蒂外，每一個人都瞭解情況。

補充

be out of the picture 不瞭解情況。

▶▶ be onto sth. 非常熟悉某事

解說

onto 在…之上，後面可接人或接物，而接人爲 be onto sb.，意思爲「非常熟悉某人」。

A：The researchers of Global Warming are really onto something.

B：Yes. They are going to be able to predict climate change.

A：全球暖化的研究者非常熟悉某事。

B：沒錯，他們能夠預測氣候改變。

bring sb. up-to-date 告訴某人最新消息

A: Can you bring me up-to-date on English class?

B: Sure. Where should I begin?

A: 你能告訴我英文課的最新消息嗎？

B: 當然可以，我要從哪裡開始呢？

catch on to 理解

必須以人當主詞。

A: Did you see Tom play baseball today?

B: Yeah, he was able to catch on to the rules of the game quite well.

A: 你今天有看到湯姆打棒球嗎？

B: 有啊，他能夠完全明白這比賽的規則。

▶▶ get through to 使…瞭解

A：It's hard for me to get through to Mary.

B：She doesn't listen to me, either.

A：要使瑪麗瞭解，對我來說很困難。
B：她也不聽我的話。

▶▶ have an eye for 懂得欣賞

A：How did you know he would be a good actor?

B：I have an eye for talent.

A：你如何知道他是一位不錯的男演員呢？
B：我懂得欣賞人才。

補充

have eyes for 是「想得到」或「對…感興趣」的意思。

figure out 弄清／理解

A：I just bought a laptop but I can't figure out how to make it work.

B：Go back to the store and get some help.

A：我剛買一台筆記型電腦，但是我無法弄懂如何操作它。

B：回到店裡去，去請人幫忙。

get the drift of 理解…含義

drift 大意、要旨。

A：I've been reading the same page for hours. I still can't get the drift of it.

B：I think you are out of it.

A：我一直在讀這一頁，好幾小時了，仍然無法理解它的含義。

B：我想你是心不在焉。

It’s all Greek to me. 我完全搞不懂

直譯爲「對我來說都是希臘語」，引申爲我完全不懂的意思。

A: Did you know the professor’s explanation?

B: It’s all Greek to me.

A: 你明白教授的解釋嗎？

B: 我完全搞不懂。

make sense out of 瞭解

A: Do you think you can make sense out of my terrible handwriting?

B: I can try.

A: 你認為你可以瞭解我潦草的筆跡嗎？

B: 我可以試看看。

miss the point 不明白

A: Why isn't Jim studying for the SAT test?

B: Maybe he's missing the point on just how important this test is.

A: 吉姆為什麼不為SAT考試用功念書呢？

B: 可能他不明白這考試的重要性。

PART

08 學習簡單與困難場景

(一) 學習簡單用語

▶▶ a piece of cake 太容易了

解說

直譯爲「一塊蛋糕」，引申爲像吃一塊蛋糕那麼容易。

A：How did you think you did on the history exam?

B：It was a piece of cake.

A：你覺得你在這次歷史考試表現得如何？

B：太容易了。

▶▶ a pushover 很容易

用在人身上，其意思爲好好先生或好好小姐；用在事物身上，其意思爲很容易的意思。

A：I need to ask for an extension on my assignment.

B: I'm sure the assignment is a pushover. You can finish it in three hours.

A: 我需要請求延期交我的作業。
B: 我確信作業是很容易的，你可以在3小時內完成它。

an easy digging 輕而易舉的事

解說

dig 有理解的意思，常用在工作或學習上。

A: The job is hard for me.

B: To me, it's an easy digging.

A: 這工作好困難啊。
B: 對我來說，它是件容易的事。

PART

child's play 容易的事

指兒童嬉戲，形容輕而易舉。

A: Can you handle this scooter?

B: I ride a scooter back home. This should be child's play.

A: 你會騎摩托車嗎？

B: 我騎一輛摩托車回家，這應該是極容易的事。

like taking candy from a baby 非常簡單

像從一個小孩子身上拿到糖果，形容某事易如反掌。

A: Do you understand how to play baseball?

B: Yes. It's like taking candy from a baby.

A：你知道如何打棒球嗎？

B：知道，它非常簡單。

形容太簡單的類似說法有：It's a breeze.，It's a snap.，It's a picnic.，It's easy.

(二) 學習困難用語

face the music 面對現實

不是面對音樂的意思，其來自於演員在登台前會緊張而忘記台詞，當音樂響起，不得不上台表演，於是必須面對現實的場面。

A：I saw Mary is looking for you.

B：I lost her notes. I guess it's time for me to face the music

A：我看見瑪麗在找你。

B：我把她的筆記弄丟了，我想該是我面對現實的時候了。

PART

hot potato 棘手問題

A：I think the broad topic of the thesis is a hot potato.

B：I think so, too. You may be biting off more than you can chew.

A：我想這廣泛的論文題目會是一個棘手問題。

B：我想也是這樣，你可能會貪多而嚼不爛。

in the hot seat 處境艱難

hot seat 困境，指在困境中須面對很多壓力。

A：I'm aware that I'm in the hot seat and need to sell my car to pay off my debts.

B：I'm sorry to hear that.

A：我察覺到我的處境艱難，必須賣掉我的車來支付債務。

B：聽到這個消息我感到很遺憾。

make trouble for sb. 給某人帶來麻煩

A：I'm afraid that Tom is making trouble for his boss.

B：Yes. He never meets his deadlines.

A：我擔心湯姆會給他的老闆帶來麻煩。
B：是啊，他未曾在期限前完成任務。

no picnic 不輕鬆

解說

指不是輕鬆愉快的事。

A：I heard your job is no picnic.

B：Well said. I never have a minute to rest.

A：我聽說你的工作並不輕鬆。
B：說得好，我從來沒有時間休息。

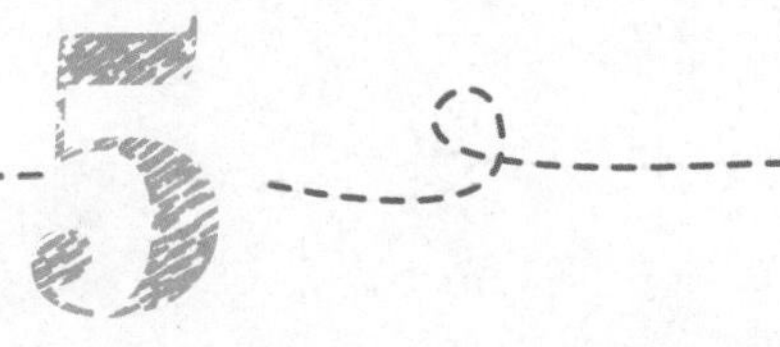
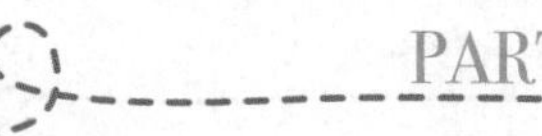

▶▶ weather the storm 度過難關

weather 平安度過。

A: The paper said that the business depression would be worse next month.

B: I've got my fingers crossed, and I hope I can weather the storm and avoid being laid off.

A: 報紙說，經濟蕭條的情形下個月會更嚴重。

B: 我必須祈禱，我希望我能度過難關和避免被解僱。

09 學習擅長與專心場景

(一) 學習擅長用語

be adept at 擅長

A：Andy is adept at playing tennis.

B：Unfortunately, the only time he can play is on Sunday afternoon.

A：安迪很擅長玩網球。

B：不幸的是，他唯一可以玩的時間是星期日下午。

be good at 擅長

A：I hope Vincent can be in our group.

B：Me, too. He seems to be naturally good at making presentations.

A：我希望文森可以加入我們這組。

B：我也一樣認為，他似乎天生很擅長做簡報。

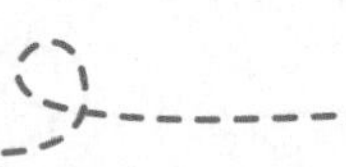

PART

be on top of sth. 熟練掌握

A: The architect Pei Ioeh Ming is on top of the design for this building.

B: I know he took part in additions to the Louvre Museum.

A: 建築師貝聿銘能熟練掌握這種建築設計。

B: 我知道他有參加羅浮宮博物館的擴建。

have a way with 擅長

way 是能力或技能。

A: Mary has a way with words.

B: I can't argue with that.

A: 瑪麗很擅長言辭。

B: 我同意。

in sb.'s element 如魚得水

形容處於適宜的環境，好像是如魚得水一般，引申爲擅長、內行或得心應手的意思。

A：I'm in my element when I enter the hockey rink.

B：How long have you played for?

A：當我進入曲棍球場時，就像是如魚得水一般。

B：你打了多久時間呢？

learn a thing or two 學會一些東西

指知道或學會一點東西。

A：How does Mark know about dinosaurs?

B：He is a student in the biology department, and learned a thing or two about paleontology.

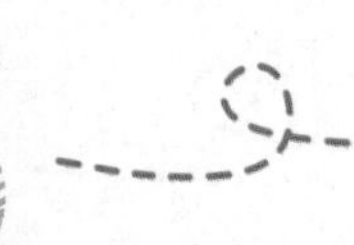

A：馬克是怎樣知道恐龍的事情呢？

B：他是一位生物系的學生，學了一些古生物學的東西。

(二) 學習專心用語

be absorbed in 全神貫注於

A：I was so absorbed in reading the novel that I lost track of time.

B：I can’t put it down as I read it.

A：我全神貫注於閱讀這本小說，以致於忘記了時間。

B：當我讀它時，我愛不釋手。

concentrate on 專心

A：I’m very tired and I can’t concentrate on my studying.

B：Maybe you should take a break before you continue studying.

A：我很累，我不能專心讀書。

B：在你繼續讀書前，或許你應該休息一下。

concentrate on = focus on

focus on 專注

指集中注意力於某事物。

A：When will your roommate be back tonight?

B：I have no idea. Now all I have to focus on is tomorrow's test.

A：你的室友今晚何時會回來？

B：我不知道，現在我所要專注的是明天的考試。

lose oneself in 專心

A: I can't lose myself in study. May I have a cup of coffee, please?

B: Yes, of course. But I don't think staying up all night will improve your chances of getting a high mark.

A: 我無法專心學習。我可以喝杯咖啡嗎？
B: 當然可以，但是我不認為整晚熬夜會提高你得到高分的機會。

pay attention 專心

A: Do you know when the test will be?

B: Didn't you pay attention in class today?

A: 你知道這次考試會在什麼時候嗎？
B: 你今天上課又不專心了？

PART

樂生活片語

01 電影場景

02 音樂場景

03 比賽場景

04 宴會場景

05 旅遊場景

06 購物場景

PART

01 電影場景

▶▶ be on 已經開始了

A：A new film is on now. Are you free to watch it?

B：I'm not sure. I am still trying to finish my homework.

A：一部新電影正在上映，你有空去看嗎？
B：我不確定，我還正努力完成我的作業。

▶▶ black and white 黑白

指色彩只有黑白顏色。

A：Do you like black and white movies?

B：They are ok, but I prefer color movies.

A：你喜歡看黑白電影嗎？
B：還可以啊，但是我較喜愛看彩色電影。

count sb. in 算某人進去

A: Would you like to go to the movies with us?

B: Count me in.

A: 你想要跟我們去看電影嗎？
B: 把我算進去。

補充

count sb. in = take sb. in

count sb. out 別把某人算在內

A: The new movie is opening tonight. Let's go and see it.

B: You'll have to count me out.

A: 今晚上演新電影，我們一起去看吧。
B: 你別把我算在內。

▶▶ leave off 中斷

指停止。

A：I couldn't finish the movie last night because I fell asleep.

B：Do you know which part you left off at?

A：我昨晚沒有看完電影，因為我睡著了。

B：你知道中斷在哪個片段嗎？

▶▶ line up for tickets 排隊買票

line up 排隊，在英國排隊用 queue。

A：What time does the movie "Harry Potter" start?

B：It will start at 7:30 sharp. After lining up for tickets, we can walk around the shopping mall.

A：電影「哈利波特」什麼時候開演呢？

B：它在7點30分準時開演。排隊買票之後，我們可以去購物中心走走。

▶▶ play up 誇大

指誇大或強調某事的重要性。

A：The previews play up the movie's plot to the audience.

B：I still think it will be nice to watch.

A：預告片會對觀衆誇大電影情節。

B：我仍然認為很值得一看。

▶▶ rave about 大肆吹捧

指極力讚賞。

PART

A: The audience was so impressed with the new movie.

B: Personally, I didn't think it was anything to rave about.

A：這部新電影給觀衆留下了深刻印象。
B：就個人而言，我覺得它不值得大肆吹捧。

save a seat 占座位

A: We will meet you at the movies ahead of time.

B: I will be late. Can you save a seat for me?

A：我們會提早在電影院和你會面。
B：我會遲到，你能為我占座位嗎？

save a seat = reserve a seat

take back 歸還

A：Did you take back the movie to the video store yet?

B：Actually, I haven't even had time to watch it.

A：你有去錄影帶店歸還這部電影嗎？
B：事實上，我還沒有時間去看它。

trade place 換座位

trade 對換，place 位置。

A：May I trade places with you?

B：Sure. It's a piece of cake.

A：我能跟你換座位嗎？
B：當然可以，小事一件。

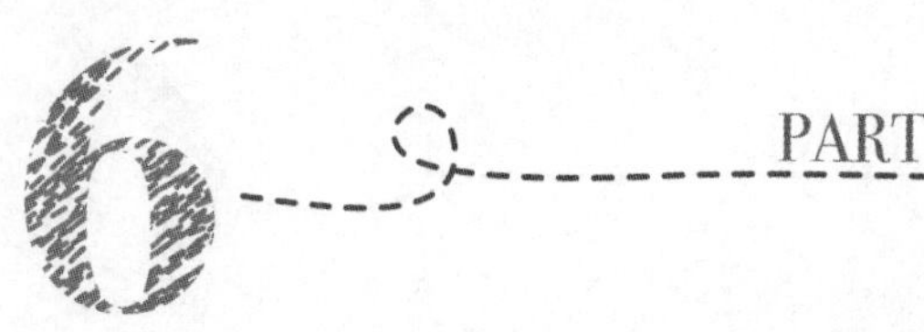

under age 未成年

A: Can I go to the movies with you?

B: The movie is for adults and you are under age.

A: 我可以跟你去看電影嗎？

B: 這部電影是給成人觀看，而你還未成年。

02 音樂場景

▶▶ aisle seat 靠走道位置

aisle 走廊、走道。

A：May I have an aisle seat, please?

B：Sorry. This concert is fully booked, so there are none available.

A：請你給我走道的位置，好嗎？

B：抱歉，音樂會已客滿，所以沒有空位了。

▶▶ be crowded with 充滿

crowd 擁擠。

A：The famous violinist is going to perform next Friday.

B：Wonderful. I think the auditorium will be

crowded with people, so we had better buy tickets in advance.

A：這位著名小提琴家將在下星期五表演。

B：太好了，我想禮堂會擠滿許多人，所以我們最好預先買票。

▸▸ be packed like sardines 非常擁擠

擁擠得像罐頭裡的沙丁魚一樣，擠得滿滿的，表示非常擁擠。

A: The concert was crowded with many people last night.

B: Yeah. They oversold the tickets and we were packed like sardines.

A：昨晚音樂會擠滿了人。

B：是啊，門票超賣，而我們被擠得像罐頭裡的沙丁魚似的。

▶▶ bring down the house 博得全場喝采

不是推倒房子，而是表演或活動叫好，而贏得大家喝采。

A：The party tonight will be awesome.

B：Yeah. We will be bringing down the house.

A：今晚宴會將會很棒。

B：沒錯，我們將會博得全場喝采。

▶▶ come out with 推出

指公開發表，而投入市場活動。

A：Adele came out with a new record.

B：I think it will be a best seller.

A：愛黛兒推出一張新唱片。

B：我想那會成為一張暢銷的唱片。

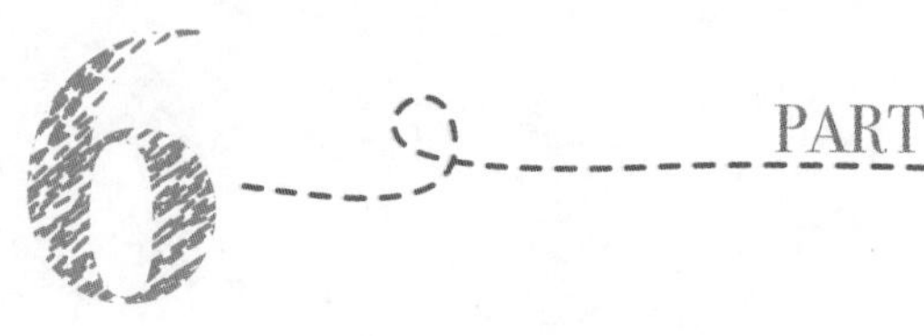

PART 6

come up 到來

解說

指即將發生或即將到來。

A: The benefit concert is coming up this week.

B: I wish I could be there.

A: 這場慈善音樂會將在這週到來。

B: 我希望我能在那裡。

have good taste in sth.

在…方面有品味

A: He has good taste in music, and he is brilliant at playing many musical instruments.

B: Yes, he is a very talented musician.

A: 他在音樂方面很有品味，而且他在演奏許多樂器上很有天分。

B: 沒錯，他是一位很有才華的音樂家。

put on 表演

A: Where are you going?

B: I'm going to the student center to put on a concert for charity.

A: 你要去哪裡呢？

B: 我要去學生活動中心為慈善音樂會表演。

put on 有「穿上」的意思，如 I put on my raincoat because it's really coming down. 因爲外面正下雨，我穿上我的雨衣。

quite a person 了不起的人

A: She not only is good at playing the violin but also can play the piano quite well.

B: She must be quite a person.

A: 她不僅擅長演奏小提琴，而且鋼琴也彈得非常好。

B: 她一定是個了不起的人。

pay off 得到好結果

指努力得到好結果。

A: He received a standing ovation from the audience after the concert.

B: I guess all his practice is finally paying off.

A: 音樂會結束後，他得到觀眾長時間起立鼓掌。

B: 我想他所有的練習終於得到好結果。

standing ovation 長時間起立鼓掌

ovation 持久的鼓掌。

A: How was Jane's concert last night?

B: It was terrific. All the audience gave her a standing ovation.

A: 昨晚珍的音樂會如何？

B: 很棒啊，所有的觀眾給了她一個長時間起立鼓掌。

▶▶ turn sb. on 喜歡

讓某人感到興趣、喜歡或感動。

A：The music is a bit tiring. Could you change it?

B：What kind of music turns you on?

A：這首音樂有點惹人煩，你能換其他音樂嗎？

B：你喜歡聽什麼音樂呢？

▶▶ wing it 即興表演

A：I like to listen to Jazz music because soloists simply wing it.

B：I wish you were a jazzman.

A：我喜歡聽爵士樂，因為獨奏者完全即興表演。

B：我希望你是一個爵士音樂家。

補充

improvise 臨時準備。

PART

03 比賽場景

▶▶ be eliminated 被淘汰

eliminate 去除。

A：Brazil versus Italy. Which team will be eliminated?

B：I think Italy will defeat Brazil.

A：巴西對抗義大利，哪一隊會被淘汰呢？

B：我認為義大利會打敗巴西。

▶▶ be good at 擅長

A：I am going to try out for the baseball team.

B：You were never that good at sports.

A：我要去參加棒球隊選拔。

B：你從來就不擅長運動。

be over 結束

A: Let's eat out tonight.

B: I'll be glad to, but after the baseball game is over.

A: 我們今晚外出吃飯吧。
B: 我很願意，不過要在棒球比賽結束後。

come in first place 獲得第一名

A: Did you hear John came in first place at the science fair?

B: Wow. He is going to be successful in his career.

A: 你有聽說約翰在科學展覽中獲得第一名？
B: 哇，他在職場上將會很成功。

compare with 與…比較

A: Do you like to watch England or Brazil play?

B: I've never watched them play, so I can't compare them.

A: 你喜歡看英國的比賽或巴西的比賽呢？
B: 我從不看它們比賽，所以我無法比較它們。

dry run 演練

指現場排演。

A: I'm very nervous that I'm giving an oral presentation tomorrow morning.

B: You should perform dry run before making your presentation.

A: 我非常緊張，我明天早上有一個口頭簡報。
B: 在你做簡報前，你應該做演練。

dry run = rehearsal

first hand 親眼

中文解說為第一手的，引申為親自看到或做到。

A：I would like to witness a baseball game first hand.

B：Let's try to buy tickets.

A：我想親眼看到棒球比賽。

B：我們想辦法去買票吧。

go on to state competition

進入州比賽

go on 繼續進行。

A：I cannot believe our basketball team went on to the state competition.

B：I believe our team is the best than it has ever been.

A：我不敢相信我們的籃球隊進入了州比賽。
B：我相信我們球隊比以往任何時候都要強。

▸▸ out of practice 久不練習

A：I saw you were a little rusty during the tennis game.

B：I'm sorry. I've been out of practice for too long.

A：我看見你在網球比賽中有點生疏。
B：我很抱歉，我很久沒有練習了。

▸▸ play-offs 季後賽

A：Are you going to watch the play-offs on television tonight?

B：You bet.

A：你今晚會看電視上的季後賽嗎？
B：當然會。

show up 出現

指露面或到達的意思。

A：I heard Bob didn't show up at the game.

B：Yes, I know. He didn't feel well, and decided to stay home.

A：我聽說鮑伯沒有出現在比賽裡。

B：是啊，我知道，他覺得不舒服，而決定留在家裡。

stand a chance 有成功的機會

A：What do you think about Brazil and Italy in the World Cup?

B：Brazil doesn't stand a chance.

A：你認為巴西與義大利的世界盃比賽誰會贏？

B：巴西沒有成功的機會。

try out for 參加選拔

指為了工作或活動而參加競爭性的測試。

A: I'm going to try out for the student's chorus.

B: Don't worry. You'll make it because you have a voice of gold.

A: 我即將去參加學生合唱團選拔。

B: 不要擔心，因為你的聲音很甜美，你會錄取的。

turn out 結果

必須經歷或測試之後，才知道的結果。

A: How is the game coming along?

B: It's done. But it didn't turn out quite like I thought.

A: 這場比賽進行的如何？

B: 它結束了，但是和我想像的結果不太一樣。

a social butterfly 交際花

直譯爲「社會蝴蝶」，形容很會交際的人，引申爲交際花。

A：I'm calling to see if she has time to help me now.

B：Save your breath. She is a social butterfly and she is going to Betty's party.

A：我想打電話給她，看看她現在是否有時間幫我的忙。

B：省省力氣吧，她是個交際花，而她正要去參加貝蒂的宴會。

break the ice 打破沉默

A：The atmosphere is quiet and serious at the party. I feel a little awkward.

B：I hope the host will soon break the ice and make the guests feel at home.

PART

A：宴會上的氣氛是安靜嚴肅，我覺得有點不自在。

B：我希望主人會很快打破沉默和讓客人覺得自在點。

count the days 期待這時刻的來臨

此片語含有渴望意思。

A：Are you eager for Christmas to arrive?

B：I'm counting the days.

A：你渴望聖誕節的來臨嗎？

B：我正期待這時刻的來臨。

have a ball 玩得開心

ball 在俚語上的意思是指愉快的時光或經歷。

A：I'm going to the party for Katherine today.

Would you like to go?

B：Sorry, I have a date with my girlfriend tonight. I am sure you'll have a ball.

A：我今晚要去參加凱薩琳的宴會，想跟我去嗎？

B：抱歉，我今晚跟女友有約，我確信你會玩得開心。

▶▶ have a good time 玩得高興

A：He said he would have a good time without you.

B：I wouldn't doubt it.

A：他說沒有你的出現，他會玩得很高興。

B：我相信。

have a good time = have a swell time = have a wonderful time

paint the town red 痛飲狂歡

指夜生活中狂歡作樂。

A: I got my first salary. Let's go and paint the town red.

B: I'd love to, but I don't even have money for a glass of beer.

A: 我拿到了我的第一份薪水，我們去痛飲狂歡吧。
B: 我很樂意去，但是我連買一杯啤酒的錢都沒有。

party animal 喜歡參加舞會的人

animal 常用來形容人有獨特才能或有特殊興趣的人。

A: I heard you are a party animal now.

B: I just love to socialize and meet new people.

A：我聽說你目前很喜歡參加舞會。

B：我只是喜歡交際和認識新朋友。

potluck party 便餐宴會

一種聚餐，每位客人各自帶食物或飲料與大家分享。

A：I wonder how many people will come to the potluck party at Helen's tonight.

B：I am not sure, but I think it would be a good idea to bring dessert.

A：我想知道今晚有多少人會在海倫家參加便餐宴會。

B：我不能確定，但是我想帶甜點是一個不錯的主意。

throw a party 舉辦宴會

較口語的說法。

A: I'm throwing a party next weekend. I wonder if you'd mind doing me a favor.

B: I'd like to, but I have a date that day.

A: 我下週末想要舉辦一個宴會，我想知道你是否介意幫我的忙。

B: 我很樂意幫忙，但是我那天有一個約會。

▶▶ take part in 參加

A: Hi, Ann, shall we take part in Janet's birthday party tonight?

B: Great idea! But we must buy a present first.

A: 嗨，安，我們今晚去參加珍妮特的生日宴會好嗎？

B: 好主意，不過我們必須先買一份禮物。

▶▶ take sb.'s time 慢慢來

A: I'll pick you up for the party now.

B：Take your time. I'm not ready yet.

A：我立刻來接你去宴會。

B：慢慢來，我還沒準備好。

out of the way 不礙事

A：Would you like to go to her party tonight?

B：I'd like to, but not until I get my paper out of the way first.

A：你今晚想去參加她的聚會嗎？

B：我樂意去，但是首先要讓我的報告不礙事。

think nothing of 別放在心上

意指沒什麼。

A：Thank you for the wonderful evening last night.

B：Think nothing of it.

PART

A：謝謝你昨晚精彩的晚會。

B：別放在心上。

▶▶ turn up 出現

A：I'm surprised that Mary didn't turn up at the party.

B：I'm sure she was interested in the party, but she probably had more important things to do.

A：我很驚訝瑪麗沒有出現在宴會上。

B：我確信她是有興趣參加宴會，但是她或許有更重要的事情要做。

05 旅遊場景

a beach person 喜歡去海灘的人

A：Would you like to join us at Miami Beach this weekend?

B：That sounds awesome. I have always been a beach person.

A：這個週末你要跟我們去邁阿密海灘嗎？

B：聽起來很棒，我總是喜歡去海灘。

口語中常用 person 來表示對某物特別喜愛，如 a movie person 喜歡看電影的人，a dog person 喜歡狗的人。

beyond compare 無與倫比

A：A trip to Alaska is too expensive for me.

B：The landscape there is beyond compare.

A：到阿拉斯加旅行對我來說是太貴了。

B：那裡的風景無與倫比。

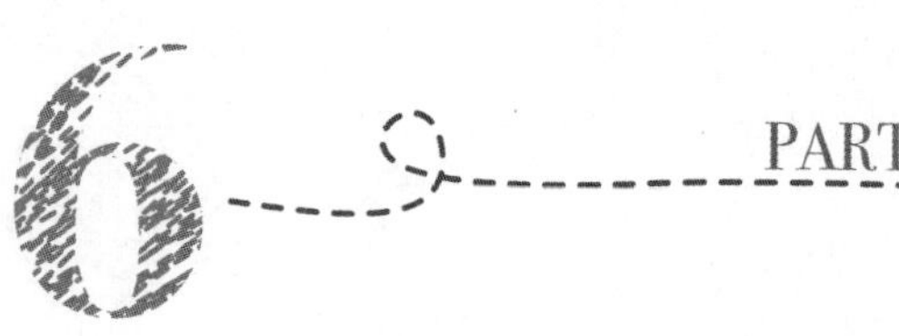

▶▶ close up 特寫

在很近的距離內拍照，指特寫。

A: I want to take a close up picture of the insect. Could you show me how?

B: You see a clear image from the lens, and then you push the button.

A: 我想要拍一張昆蟲特寫，你能教我方法嗎？

B: 你從鏡頭看到清晰的影像，然後你就按下按鈕。

▶▶ in season 旺季

A: Traveling costs are more in season.

B: You said it. Hotels are always so expensive.

A: 在旺季時旅行費用較貴。

B: 你說得對，旅館總是很貴。

off-season 淡季

A：Let's go see the pyramids in Egypt.

B：Not now. The airfare is dirt cheap during the off-season.

A：我們去埃及看金字塔吧。

B：不要現在，飛機票在淡季是非常便宜的。

take a holiday 度假

A：We've both been working too hard lately.

B：I'll say. Let's have next week off and take a holiday.

A：最近我們兩個工作的太辛苦了。

B：我同意，我們下週休假去度假吧。

take a holiday = have a holiday

PART 6

▸▸ sleep on 考慮一晚

解說

把問題留在第二天解決，指需要考慮。

A：Would you like to go camping this weekend?

B：Maybe, let me sleep on it.

A：這個週末你想要去露營嗎？

B：或許吧，讓我考慮一晚。

▸▸ take a picture 拍照

A：The view is spectacular. Do you mind taking a picture of me in the background?

B：Of course not.

A：這一帶風景很壯觀，你介意以這為背景幫我拍照嗎？

B：當然不介意。

picture = shot

▶▶ take sb.'s breath away 使某人大吃一驚

中文意思爲帶走某人的呼吸，引申爲使某人大吃一驚。

A: What did you think of the Yosemite?

B: That place was so beautiful that it took my breath away.

A: 你覺得優勝美地國家公園怎麼樣呢？

B: 那地方很漂亮，以致於它讓我大吃一驚。（暗示風景漂亮）

▶▶ take out of 拿出

A: Tom, the landscape is so beautiful.

B: Yes, now I want to take my camera out of my backpack to take some photos.

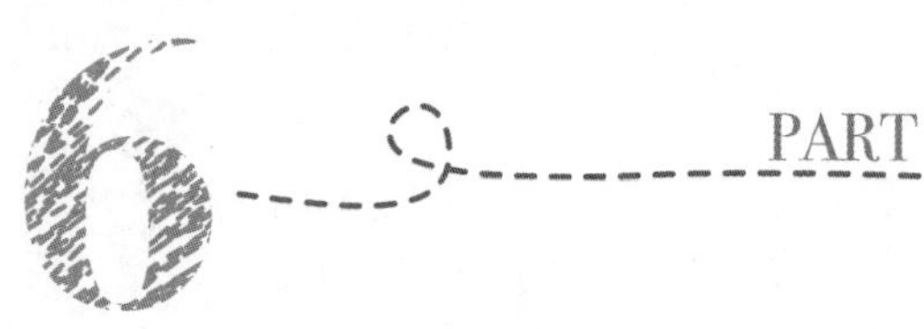

A：湯姆，這風景很漂亮。

B：對啊，現在我想要拿出我的後背包裡面的相機來拍一些照片。

▶▶ tourist trap 敲觀光客竹槓的地方

A：The souvenirs and food are so expensive close to the beach.

B：That's because the tourist traps are located close to the beaches.

A：靠近海灘附近的紀念品和食物是很貴的。

B：那是因為敲詐觀光客的地方是位於海灘附近。

▶▶ under exposed 曝光不足

A：Can you take a picture of me with the waterfall as the background?

B：I'm afraid the picture will be under exposed because I didn't take the flash with me today.

A：以瀑布為背景，你可以幫我拍照嗎？

B：我怕這張相片會曝光不足，因為我今天沒隨身帶閃光燈。

over exposed 過度曝光。

06 購物場景

a great deal 真划算

A：If you buy one book, you get one free.

B：That's a great deal.

A：這書是買一送一。

B：真划算。

for free 免費

A：If I purchase the stereo, the salesman said I could have the headphones for free.

B：That sounds like a really good deal.

A：如果我買這台音響，售貨員說我可以得到免費耳機。

B：聽起來像是很好的交易。

grocery shopping 採購日用品

A: Could you lend me your car to go grocery shopping?

B: Sorry. I don't like to let anyone else drive my car. My insurance only covers me.

A: 你的車子能借給我去採購日用品嗎？

B: 抱歉，我不喜歡讓其他人開我的車，我的保險只適用我。

knock off 減少

常指價格上的降低。

A: The price is a bit steep. Will you knock off another 20 dollars?

B: You can't haggle as it's a fixed price.

A: 這價錢有點貴，你能再便宜20美元嗎？

B: 你不能討價還價，因為它是不二價。

shop around 貨比三家

指逛商店要多逛幾家，以比較商品價格、品質或款式。

A: I want to buy that cell phone. But the price is a little expensive.

B: You should shop around before you buy it. You shouldn't be an impulse buyer.

A: 我想要買那支手機，但是價格稍微貴了點。

B: 你買它之前，最好能貨比三家，別當一個衝動的購買者。

two for one 買一送一

A: All coffees are on sale today.

B: Are they two for one?

A: 今天所有咖啡特價中。

B: 它們是買一送一嗎？

two for one = buy one get one free 買一送一；two to one 二對一；kill two birds with one stone 一石二鳥。

window shopping 逛街

只逛不買東西。

A：Let's go window shopping.

B：I know there is a nice place to stroll on Broadway.

A：我們去逛街吧。

B：我知道在百老匯有一個閒逛的好地方。

國家圖書館出版品預行編目資料

口說日常生活英文片語會話／王仁癸著. --初版. --臺北市：書泉, 2014.07

面； 公分

ISBN 978-986-121-930-1 (平裝附光碟片)

1.英語 2.會話 3.慣用語

805.188 103010209

3AN7

口說日常生活英文片語會話

作　　者— 王仁癸(17.4)

發 行 人— 楊榮川

總 編 輯— 王翠華

主　　編— 朱曉蘋

責任編輯— 吳雨潔

封面設計— 吳佳臻

出 版 者— 書泉出版社

地　　址：106台北市大安區和平東路二段339號4樓

電　　話：(02)2705-5066　傳　　真：(02)2706-6100

網　　址：http://www.wunan.com.tw

電子郵件：shuchuan@shuchuan.com.tw

劃撥帳號：01303853

戶　　名：書泉出版社

經 銷 商：朝日文化

進退貨地址：新北市中和區橋安街15巷1號7樓

TEL：(02)2249-7714　FAX：(02)2249-8715

法律顧問　林勝安律師事務所　林勝安律師

出版日期　2014年7月初版一刷

定　　價　新臺幣420元